DATRA *the muskrat*

AT THE POND, VOLUME III

by Franklin Russell
illustrated by Richard Cuffari

DATRA *the muskrat*

FOUR WINDS PRESS   NEW YORK

By the same author

ARGEN THE GULL
THE FRIGHTENED HARE
HAWK IN THE SKY
THE HONEYBEES
SEARCHERS AT THE GULF
THE SECRET ISLANDS
WATCHERS AT THE POND
CORVUS THE CROW
LOTOR THE RACCOON

Published by Four Winds Press
A Division of Scholastic Magazines, Inc., New York, N.Y.
Copyright © 1972 by Franklin Russell
Illustrations © 1972 by Scholastic Magazines, Inc.
All rights reserved.
Printed in the United States of America
Library of Congress Catalogue Card Number: 72-77813

CHAPTER I

Datra swam to the bottom of the pond. There, the thickness of the surface ice had cut the light to a faint glow, and most of the oxygen-producing plant photosynthesis had stopped. The fish, which had gone half to sleep on the bottom, were slowly suffocating as the scarce oxygen supply was used up by the rotting vegetation. Datra saw them clustered together, their gills moving slowly, their tails and fins practically motionless.

In his underwater swimming, Datra passed many of the other pond creatures, all surviving in their separate ways. Dragonfly nymphs lay semi-dormant, awaiting the time when they would be transformed into fragile, flying insects. The water beetles, black-backed, spotted golden, common almost everywhere in stream and pond and marsh, had been driven by the scarcity of oxygen to cling to the few green plants that still survived beneath the ice. In the southern part of the pond where the ice was more than a foot thick, many of the beetles swam in colonies, searching for pockets of oxygen. Unlike the fish, they could stand being frozen solid and could survive this oxygen shortage for a long time.

As he kicked up puffs of silt with his powerful back legs, Datra saw perch darting away from his nose. Their stomachs had shrunk to help them survive the winter, and they were sleepy, but they kept hunting, kept searching for the nymphs which were hiding below in the mud.

Datra was the perfect aquatic animal, a deep-chested, thickly furred muskrat, who could stay under water for fifteen minutes, but the cold was beginning to hurt him too. He had gone into the winter with reserves of food in his pond-side lodge. He had not been troubled by the thickening ice. He was a powerful swimmer and he did not panic during underwater emergencies. Often, swimming far under the ice, he would find one of his exit holes to the surface blocked. But even with more than half his oxygen supply gone, he remained calm and investigated the area to see whether or not there was a chance of reaching the surface through any other old hole. He knew to the second how long the air in his lungs would last. He swam without haste, without panic, and thus conserved his two most valuable resources—his muscular energy and his oxygen—until he found a free hole or chopped his way to the surface.

His body was plump and the dark brown fur on it was so

dense that the shiny ends matted whenever he left the water. But the inner fur near his body remained dry. His belly fur was gray; and his face though shorter and broader than that of a true rat, was whiskered. His eyes were large and brown, and his scaly tail, flattened on both sides, stretched more than seven inches from his body. Lead-colored scars of old wounds pocked his body. His rump was gouged where another muskrat had neatly bitten out a ball of flesh. His left ear had been ripped by a great horned owl when Datra once fled into the safety of the pond. Long-healed gashes crisscrossed his flanks.

Datra looked more mouse-like than rat-like, but no mouse ever grew to his size. He was nearly as large as a small rabbit—a giant among muskrats. He kicked his four-pound body through the water by powerful hind feet which were partially webbed. He used his tail as a sinuous rudder to guide him and help him through the masses of rubbish on the bottom of the winter pond.

He was the perfect underwater hunter, but his teeth were his most superb weapon of offense, defense, and work. Even the vicious mink, longer than Datra, feared these teeth, and sometimes the big red fox drew back when Datra rose, chattering rage, and bared the long, curving, cutting weapons. His teeth could bite deep enough to kill another muskrat. They were supremely suitable for digging underwater, for rooting out the stems of plants frozen in ice, and for chopping meals from the living stalks of burweeds and cattails. With them, Datra could slash upward through the solid ice.

Whether or not Datra lived well—or poorly—in the icebound pond depended on the bounty of the previous summer and the severity of the current winter. There were many foods in the winter pond, some of them not obvious. There were nuts and seeds and berries, fallen into the pond in the autumn. There were the roots of blue flags and cattails and arrowheads. There were dormant plant lice caught exposed on various plants, and countless other hibernating insects. The food was there for those who were able to find it.

As Datra swam along, he appeared to be in an icy prison, but the pond was endlessly replenished by the small amount of water still flowing into it under the ice. Snails and small entomostracans and algae were all able to play out winter lives with hardly a pause. The meat-hunting planarian worms shot their tiny bodies through the dusky water in search of food. The larval forms of the summer insects moved slowly across the rocks and grazed on the algae that was growing there.

Datra had survived five years because he was experienced and tough, and he knew the pond like no other muskrat. He lived where others died. Earlier this winter, he had swum to the far western end of the pond, mostly unknown territory for him, and had cautiously entered another lodge where he had once been welcomed. He had found nothing but silence, the lodge filled with more than twenty muskrats, all of them lying silent and unmoving, dead and frozen. Twice before, swimming deeply under the ice where shafts of dim light came through rifts, he had seen muskrats frozen into the ice above him, the dark shapes seeming to float in mid-distance. Sometimes, as he swam, he heard the sound of tiny, tapping noises far away. When he came nearer, he saw the black shape of a hungry crow trying to dig through the ice to reach the frozen animals.

Datra's world was the pond, now a silent and frozen place, but in summer it sparkled like a jewel in the necklace of marsh and pool and bog which adorned the country running east to the sea. Water from immense reaches of northern forest came quietly down and emptied itself into the flat, wet lands. Tiny streams ran alongside banks of turf. The water reached gradually from level to level and passed through the pond to find an eager, tree-flanked stream. Then it tumbled off to a southern river valley.

Datra's pond was set among other watering places, themselves all former ponds but now mostly filled in by the ceaseless victories of grass, aquatic plants, trees and shrubs. They had become marsh-like places that would soon be dry land. His pond was the last hold-out, the deepest and broadest tract of water resting easily in its still-unfilled basin. The silt was deep at its bottom, true, but this created a perfect refuge for all kinds of life. A small island rested in the center of the pond.

To the east lay the great marsh which hosted many thousands of muskrats. Datra knew it well; he had been there often and had hunted among the arrowheads and water plantains, the bulrushes and burweeds, the water horsetails and pickerel weeds, the docks and loosestrifes, but he preferred the contained world of the pond which he knew intimately.

The marsh teemed with life, and Datra knew of its catfish and suckers, its minnows and golden shiners, silverfins

and eels. But in the pond, he was more easily master of his world. The great horned owl, one of his deadliest enemies, hunted most often in the marsh. The marsh drew hawks and gulls, owls and mink, skunks and weasels and foxes. Datra, in his way, lived in the safer place.

He swam now toward the southern limits of the pond. The mud shelved and the matted vegetation thickened as the water became more shallow. Eventually he stopped at the point where mud and ice converged. He knew that often this was a good place to find victims of the winter, fish which had been unable to withstand suffocation and had swum or floated upward to this point of no return. Here was the place where aquatic insects, also seeking escape, came and burrowed shallowly in the mud. Datra snuffled in the muddy bottom, his back bumping the ice. He had lived long enough to know that no winter was ever like any other, and he always hunted hard and long. He knew that abundance could change to scarcity in a day.

Once, many years before, during an extremely easy winter, an unexpectedly savage freeze had struck. In eight days it froze his territory clear down to the muddy bottom of the water. He had chiseled away at his lodge's exit and entrance holes, but the ice gradually reached beneath his house. His plunge holes, leading to his stock of buried roots, were soon all sealed off. He quickly became desperately hungry. At first, he ate all the edible plant material in the lodge itself, picking over every scrap of material that had the faintest food value. Then, forcing through the last hole that led up through the ice, he had gone into the open and tried foraging about the wreckage of last summer's plants. He had even made two reluctant forays up into the trees. But that was strange and frightening territory for him and he had soon returned to the pond.

As hunger and desperation increased, he had chiseled scraps of frozen fish out of the ice. He had eaten dried grass. He had gnawed at old bones and the dried skin of a rabbit. All around him, other muskrats were starving to death, or fleeing to unknown fates beyond the pond and marsh. He had one memory of a female, sprawled out on the ice of the pond, still alive, but dying. The freeze was blinding—her eyes were frozen shut. When Datra approached, she lifted her head and sniffed the air as though sensing the approach of a friend. But it was not Datra she sought, and her head dropped hopelessly.

Datra had survived that winter, thin and weak, but he had never forgotten the bad time. This one was much easier, at least so far. Now, with his oxygen supply at the halfway mark, he turned from the ice and mud and headed back toward his lodge, his back bumping under the ice.

The lodge loomed up, a great mass of twined sticks, grasses, chunks of mud, all bound together to form a sprawling shelter that reached from the muddy shallows up into the ice, and beyond it to the surface. Datra had drilled tunnels in the side of the lodge. He entered one of these and crawled up through its black twists and turns until he came out of the water and entered the main chamber of the lodge. There, on a mat of half-frozen vegetation that made up the floor, he stretched himself slightly, muzzle down, feet curled under his body, and went to sleep.

Over the next few days, the cold deepened intensely around Datra's lodge. By the fifth day, he sensed a crisis. The ice gripped all his entrances and exits, clogged the long, deep plunge channel that led away to the center of the pond, and threatened, on this day, to freeze his entire lodge.

He might withstand the attack of winter if he could remain active and chew away the encroaching ice that was reaching for him. But he must have food, and the supply was running short. By the eighth day of the freeze, the two main food rooms in the lodge were empty. The third and fourth rooms contained only some scraps of root stalks. Datra moved uneasily around his central chamber, feeling the cold seeping through its walls. The warmth of his body melted the ice, and moisture from his breathing condensed and dripped on him. He must move soon, but experience warned him that the open ice was now the most dangerous place on earth for a muskrat.

On the ninth day of the freeze, he knew he must move or die. He felt his way down the corridor toward the plunge hole. It was frozen solid. If the ice had reached so far beneath the lodge, he had little chance of digging through it. Even if he were able to hack through such thick ice and reach unfrozen water beneath, he would still have to dig up through the ice to reach the surface. His body was best fitted for digging upward, not for gouging downward. After nuzzling the ice in the channel for a few seconds, he turned back toward his imprisonment in the main chamber of the lodge.

Then, without hesitation, he chiseled into the wall of the chamber itself, his digging aimed at the short side of the lodge. The central chamber was not located exactly in the middle of the lodge, and because it was only inches above the water level, Datra angled his digging slightly upward to bring him out just above the level of the ice outside. His large teeth slashed slivers of ice away, ripped and pulled at the frozen vegetation, at the small stones and chunks of frozen mud, kicking it all behind him into the lodge chamber.

So well was he master of this black world of ice and freezing cold that he felt no concern, no panic. He had no doubts about his ability to escape. He worked for an hour, now half-buried in the debris of his own digging, before he saw the gloom ahead changing as light filtered through the ice. He paused and heard the wind cutting a mournful tune outside. With one last, cautious effort, he burst through the outermost layer of the wall, fought his way through a bank of snow lying beyond it, and then stood upright, whiskers trembling, looking out across the pond.

Complete desolation swept away on all sides. A great storm, the sounds of which had come only dimly to him, had coated everything thickly in white. Snow had been driven into mountainous drifts and great weights of ice bowed the trees. The pond did not look like the place where Datra had begun his winter. The wind was merciless. It sped across the pond and Datra felt moisture freezing around his eyes, felt the con-

densed wet on his belly and paws turning to ice. He knew
he could not long survive in the open. He turned toward the
northern shore of the pond, his feet breaking through the
snow crust in places. A quickly thickening flurry of snow
flakes began to fall. This was no time for a muskrat to be
aground. This was no place for a creature whose safety depended on deep water and submarine food. Now he was
forced to move on, hoping to find food before he froze.

At the northern shore of the pond, where the snow was
very thick, he paused, and saw another creature. A crow
stood in a branch overhead, peering forward uncertainly
into the force of the wind and shaking snowflakes from his
eyes. The crow was as hungry as Datra. He had not fed
that day and had eaten only poorly the previous day. He,
much more than Datra, needed regular food to keep alive.
As Datra watched, the crow shook himself and stropped his
beak on a branch. Then he turned to an entrance hole in the
tree trunk and poked in. He leaped back when the crusted
snow burst in his face. Datra, not concerned with crows, began moving into the woods. He did not see that the crow had
disturbed a sleeping raccoon in her refuge hole in the hollow
tree. As Datra loped clumsily along, turning one way and
then another, the crow took wing with one big cry and disappeared against the force of the searching wind.

Datra paused at a small, spherical hole in the snow. Smelling something, he dug down cautiously and found a pellet
bound together with frozen grass. Inside was a collection of
small bones, the husks of seeds, and other pieces of undi-

gested food the crow had eaten the day before. He had spat out all the pieces he could not digest. Now, Datra methodically pulled the pellet to pieces and tried to find something for himself. He chewed some of the seed husks, nibbled at some of the bones, but it was a futile task.

Ahead, the woods lay silent for a moment in a lull in the wind. Then the topmost branches sighed and rattled and the wind roared distantly as it touched other parts of the forest, sweeping up the snow. Datra shivered. Impulsively, he began digging into the side of a deep drift of snow.

Datra could survive on almost any scrap of vegetation he might find, even pieces of frozen green grass, or the stalks of old weeds, or occasional nuts or seeds. But others had already searched in this alien territory. Nevertheless, he continued to dig. His long, flat tail disappeared behind him into the snow bank, and the snow fell and concealed his digging.

Datra, with great luck, was digging straight toward food. Before the snowstorm, a squirrel's nest in the fork of a tree had been torn loose by the wind. It was filled with nuts stored by its prudent builder to get through the winter. But when the snow followed so quickly after the wind, it was buried with no trace. Datra's digging feet ripped away the dried grasses and quickly laid bare its store of beechnuts, walnuts, acorns and other tree seeds. He gorged.

Before dusk, he was back in the security of his lodge, his exit tunnel plugged with snow, shards of ice, chunks of mud and vegetation. He lay on the icy floor, the water dripping around him again, and slept the sleep of the contented. Outside, his hungry enemies circled the frozen pond, and waited.

CHAPTER II

To have a full stomach, to lie contented and asleep in the lodge, to dream away the bad times of winter—these were fleeting moments in Datra's winter life. Sleep was one way of surviving the winter; sleep and sleep again, all bodily functions slowed. But sleep was an illusion. Although he had no need to chase food as a crow or a fox did, he still must eat to survive. He could not go into a sleep as deep as that of the raccoon or skunk, so Datra compromised. He slept long and ate little. But now, each awakening was more unpleasant than the last.

His fight for survival grew more difficult, but his spirit remained resilient and aggressive. He accepted the snow now as his hunting ground. He was the only surviving muskrat

at the pond, and he was a favorite target for owls, minks, foxes, weasels and hawks. Every moment ashore was risky, but he had no choice because there was the center of the great mouse hunt.

The mice were everywhere. Each drift of snow had its base riddled with a hundred zigzagging tunnels cut into the dry-grass debris of the previous summer. The tunnels cut through ice and mud, moved through the trunks of fallen trees, and into the ground, then out again. The mice were so numerous that in places along the pond's shores, where snow and dried vegetation melded with the water ice, they had drowned as they burrowed furiously in search of seeds, dried fruits and sleeping insects.

On the third day of his snow-hunting, while Datra was crouched half inside a hollow tree, two playful weasels whisked past him, one chasing the other. The first weasel dived into a snowbank, and the other followed, both emerging in an explosion of snow with the female holding a squealing mouse in her mouth. When the weasels had disappeared,

a great black crow came planing down and searched through the snow for another mouse. He, too, finally made his kill and flew off to a nearby tree with a mouse wriggling in his beak.

Datra could not equal such skill, but he could dig. Methodically, he worked his way from one end of the snowbank to the other. The smell of mice was everywhere. Datra, in his clumsy searching, caused the tunnels to collapse all around him. When he finally came near a mouse, his frantic victim could not dig free, and Datra pushed forward and killed with one quick bite.

In this bad time, the hunting was never good. Datra had to range across the ice and into the woods and nearby streams for food. He moved down beneath the ice smothering the southern exit stream from the pond, and worked his way cautiously along the gravelled bottom in search of insect larvae fastened to stones, or wedged between boulders, or buried in mud. He dug sleeping crayfish from their submarine burrows, ate snails and sleepy water insects resting on the bottom. No scrap of food was too small for his eager teeth.

Datra knew that every moment was potentially dangerous. The freezing weather made even his daily return to the lodge chancy; sometimes he would find the lodge entrance thickly iced over. One day the movements of a mink, and the flight of a huge white owl forced him into the thin protection of snow-covered shrubbery and he could not return to his lodge until late dusk.

The afternoon had been freezing. The ice had moved several inches across the full width of the pond and buckled near his lodge. Datra, cold and hungry, at first could not find the entrance at all. Then he scented it along the broken line of the ice-buckle. He tried to dig there, but the movement of the ice had crushed the thinner, newer ice of the entrance into smithereens. Then he tried to bite his way down through some old, rock-hard ice which had been pulverized and compressed.

His digging efforts became feeble when he realized the futility of his work. Frightened now, he bounded like a miniature kangaroo across the pond to another, very old plunge hole, long since permanently sealed by the ice. He scrabbled away the snow and began to bite downward. But this effort was even more futile, even more pathetic, since it was based on a failing memory: the hole was thickly sealed. He stood up, whiskers twitching, and the muffled *hooing* cry of the great horned owl came rolling in from the distance.

Galvanized again, Datra bounded back across the pond to his lodge. He scraped the snow away from the buckle in the ice. Bracing his feet, he began gouging inward. He was more determined now, but still panicky. His other two failures worked against his determination, and he could not get the leverage he needed to dig well. Once, years before, he had joined another equally desperate muskrat in an effort to regain the security of a lodge and had worked beside the other animal for an hour. But the other muskrat, older and less forceful than Datra, had become discouraged. With his body two-thirds out of sight, his long tail curved snake-like on the chipped debris of his digging, he had stopped. Datra, digging a parallel tunnel under exactly the same conditions, had never doubted his ability to get into the lodge. He had not stopped, and had broken into the central chamber just as the other creature died.

But now, Datra was much older. He had suffered many disappointments. He no longer had the same heedless, blind determination of the young. He was inclined to remember his failures. Now, quite suddenly, he slowed his digging. Dusk had passed. Bright moonlight glittered across the pond. The great owl call was much closer and might mean that the huge bird was at the fringe of the pond itself. Perhaps it was Datra's exhaustion that stopped his digging. Perhaps he understood instinctively that he did not have the strength to reach the chamber of the lodge. Whatever the reason, he backed out of the hole and turned his face to the moonlit pond, his eyes bright for a sign of the owl. Cautiously, not bounding now, he began to work his way east along the fringes of the pond.

He was possessed by an old memory of a time when he had narrowly escaped dying. Memory often burns brightest in older lives, making it possible to choose between one act and another. Datra *remembered* how once, in such a crisis, he had saved his life.

He knew that shelter meant many things, depending on

the degree of cold, on the strength of the wind, on the damp-
ness or dryness of the air. The air was bitterly cold, but it
was still, and he understood that if he could find a simple
shelter, enough to contain the warmth of his own body,
enough to conceal him from his enemies, he might get
through the night. He rummaged through the wreckage of
some cattails, trying to sweep debris together into a pile big
enough to cover him, but the effort failed.

He retreated further, moving toward the easternmost end
of the pond and clinging to its northern shores. There, two
sharp-backed ridges of snow had been wind-driven behind
the lee of a fallen tree trunk. Finally, inside one of these
drifts, Datra found his shelter, digging into it as though he
were burrowing into the black earth of autumn. He lived inside this snow bank for two days until a slight thaw unlocked
the ice grip on his lodge. Working at dusk, he opened plunge
holes and returned to the bottom of the pond, and then into
his lodge.

The freezes in Datra's absence and, now, the condensa-
tion of his moist breath on the walls around him combined
to make the chamber only a little bigger than the size of his
own body. The ceiling had dropped until its lowest point
touched his head. The coating of ice on the chamber walls
was now so dense that practically no air penetrated through
them from outside. Yet Datra could survive in the lodge.
His skills at survival were not especially dramatic, but they
were always critical. His lungs, choked with hydrogen sulfide

and the gases of decomposition, could still breathe and re-breathe the disappearing oxygen.

When he lay in the lodge chamber, sometimes for two days or more without stirring, his breathing was slow and shallow. Sometimes, the air became too foul, even for him, and he would move to his exit hole and chop his way through the icy matrix of vegetation and mud until he reached the clean fresh air outside.

The pond was so thoroughly locked into the middle of winter that no hint of spring was visible anywhere. Datra survived, a breath at a time, while all around him the winter eliminated creatures by the scores, by the hundreds. Yet within the pond, now a very dark and dusky gray, a great resurgence of new life was beginning to take place. While Datra suffered in his stinking lodge, other creatures were preparing themselves for the great race into the sun. Larval salamanders and bullfrog tadpoles were growing quickly. Aquatic dragonflies, caddisflies and craneflies were also growing, as though spring had already arrived. Tiny mites teemed in parts of the pond, some of them hosted by the breathing mussels. Pushing at the ice, thousands of crustaceans seemed to be trying to force their way out. At one place along the western shore, crayfish paired in scores amidst dark, bubbling water moving underneath the ice. Pairs of fairy shrimp danced under the thickest pond ice, their brood pouches already filled with embryos. Water fleas, ready for the thaw, swarmed under the ice, their brood pouches full. Stoneflies, oblivious to the ice, came through it somehow and moved out of the pond, their aquatic bodies looking strange in the chill air. They crawled over sparkling snow, ready to assume their winged forms.

Datra, who caught some of the stoneflies and ate them, still had no recognition of the imminence of spring. He was given no external stimulus that would push him forward into a new season. Indeed, at this critical time, when the seasons were changing, many creatures like him were dying, as though there were a dividing line of stress running between winter and spring. As a non-sleeping resident of the winter pond, Datra was more like the star-nosed moles who had also endured the ice and snow without sleeping. They had dug through the snow, drilled tunnels through solid ice, and swum deeply in the ice-covered pond. They were constant, dangerous enemies of small, drowsing fish.

But Datra's time was near.

Although the ice showed no sign of melting, his spring season began one morning when he came out of his lodge and looked across the frozen pond. Everything lay as still as death. The drag marks of some mink victim passed nearby. The sun sparkled through twigs encased in sheaths of ice. Yet this morning, Datra could feel the new season stirring in his body as the many changes in his glands began the work of transforming both his self-identity and his body. He felt a rising irritation at the sight of a mink sliding through the cattail wreckage to the east. His immediate impulse was to run out and attack the lithe form, to drive it from the pond completely. He had a strong sense of territory. The irritation passed slowly, becoming sharp again when a blizzard struck the pond. But the storm passed and left in its aftermath a stronger, warmer sun.

In the marsh, the other muskrats felt the new season as well. Some of them, a few of the more adventurous, left the marsh and crossed the pond in search of new spring places. Now, Datra's feeling of territory became dominant. As the interlopers passed through his land, he chased any who paused, however briefly, near his place. He drove all the passing muskrats to the farthest reaches of the western pond, or down the exit stream to the south.

His new mood was confirmed by a change in the air. One early morning, long before dawn, he heard the sound of thaw beyond the lodge. At first, it was only a whisper of running water that soon became a hiss of dark snow-water riding over ice. Inside the lodge, his tiny room rained large drops of water. When Datra came out at dawn and viewed the thawing pond, he saw it gleaming with a shining new surface of melted snow. The sound of rushing water hissed and roared from the woods. He loped forward, picking up worms and beetles and larvae washed free by the thawing waters. He saw other muskrats moving across the pond surface, hunched black marks pushing steadily forward.

Although the thaw seemed positive, and the air was now warm enough for spring, Datra remained cautious. When he returned to his lodge, he chiseled ice from its roof, dug down into the muck of its floor, and tried to bring up scattered pieces of vegetation. That night, lying half-submerged in melted water, he felt a new chill stealing in through the walls. Outside, the moon shone through a sky almost completely shrouded in clouds, and a great cold settled over the pond. It came down and reached among the trees. It froze millions of incautious creatures who had emerged from their winter sleep prematurely.

When Datra stirred himself next morning, he had to chisel his way out through fresh ice, and break from the lodge in a shower of ice splinters. He looked doubtfully out onto a pond made cold and silent again. The freeze had come back so swiftly that it had caught many in its path. Before him on the ice a wasp stood immobilized by the cold, scarcely able to move any of her limbs. On the far side of the pond, Datra could see another muskrat trying to claw into the ice blocking the entrance to a mounded lodge.

He looked overhead and saw a crow wheeling back and forth, like a hawk, and heard the dreaded cry of the great owl in the distance. He listened intently but the cry did not come again. He began to lick his front feet. The wind was bitter in his eyes, not blowing hard, but icy cold. And Datra stood there, unmoving, his memory of the past faulty for one moment. When he decided to travel across the ice to the wreckage of the cattails, he found he could not move. At first, he was angry. After all his caution, his tail was stuck

fast to the new ice. Not calm now, he tugged and jerked
without success.

His struggles attracted the crow who came down in wide
circles and landed nearby. Datra looked warily at him, and
stopped his struggling for a moment. But when the crow
walked toward him, beady black eyes gleaming, Datra knew
he was an enemy. He stood up as tall as possible, showed his
long teeth, and chattered with rage. The crow watched doubtfully for a moment, then turned away, walking toward the
icy shore, and there hammered at a frozen toad in the new
ice.

After another hour of struggle, Datra heard the great owl
calling again, this time much closer. He gave up and crouched
down, waiting.

CHAPTER III

Some muskrats, their tails frozen to the ice, escaped by chewing them off. Datra had seen animals with only stumps for tails. But now, in this agony of waiting, it never occurred to him to try and gnaw through the base of his tail. Instead, he waited, even though he knew that he was defenseless against owl, or fox, or raccoon, or mink.

Soon after midday, he saw a large bird flying south of the pond, and he crouched down. The bird disappeared. A slight change in the air told Datra to keep waiting, and in time warm air began moving in over the pond. With a deft twist, Datra freed himself and slipped away back to his lodge. As he disappeared, the great horned owl came across the pond on silent wings.

When the real thaw began that night, its sound had a new quality. Datra felt the lodge trembling in the grip of rushing waters, heard the grind and snap of branches torn off dead trees. He moved uneasily, remembering a time many years ago when his lodge had been carried away in a spring flood. Trapped inside, all the exits broken up, he had been rolled over and over until the lodge was smashed in fast-running rapids, and he had found himself spilled out into midnight-black water in a forest stream.

But this lodge was the most secure he had ever built. He had added to it over the years, and it was enormous, towering more than four feet above the water. Food-storage chambers and rooms for suckling young were built around the central chamber where he bedded a few inches above the water. The rooms were connected by tunnels, and three plunge holes led outward from the central chamber through the submerged base, which was fastened to the bottom of the pond by a strong mixture of silt, the roots of old sweet flags, willow shoots and other aquatic vegetation.

With its corridors, chambers, and underwater exits, it was so big that Datra often could not keep it solely for himself. Other muskrats came into it and sometimes used it for days before he even knew they were there.

The lodge trembled but was too firmly fixed to be carried away. Instead, Datra heard the rising waters coming up the plunge hole corridors, heard the echoing slap and gurgle of water in them. He decided to leave the lodge and see what was happening outside. But when he plunged into the hole, he found the corridor already choked with debris. It was too loose for him to dig through, and too tight for him to force through. Even as he struggled downward, he could feel more debris gathering behind him. He tried to back up, since he could not turn in the narrow corridor, but this, too, proved to be impossible.

A faint edge of desperation touched his movements now as he twisted his body and bit into the debris of the tunnel wall. A dozen slashes of his powerful teeth loosened more debris, which continued to gather around him, making it even more difficult to move. But now he was able to turn. Immediately, he attacked the debris that had gathered behind him. This was loosely set in the water and after five hard minutes, with his air reserve almost exhausted, he chopped his way through the last of it, burst out of the water, back into the lodge's central chamber, and lay there, panting.

The water kept rising until it reached into the lodge's main room. Now Datra faced the very real risk of drowning in his own home. He went quickly to work, standing up on powerful back legs and gnawing at the ceiling of the room. He tore down grass and sticks and balls of mud which splashed into the water around him. Here the digging was easier, and in half an hour he broke through the roof of the lodge and stood there in the roaring darkness.

All around him sounds of distress and crisis pierced the night air. Heavy rain lashed his muzzle and he heard the choking croak of a crow which had somehow become caught up in the flood waters. The dim shape of a raccoon raced by. She was clinging desperately to a log. Datra knew from his experience that the water carried many helpless victims of the flood. Af if to confirm his memory, a dead mouse floated past.

The lodge shook under his feet, and after a moment's hesitation, he plunged into the black waters and swam toward

the northern shores of the pond, where he found shelter inside a hollow, fallen tree.

Datra's lodge was strongly built, but the lodges of less careful muskrats were not so secure. The waters of the pond and marsh rose; and the skill of the muskrats as builders was tested. Some were found wanting. The rising waters ripped many lodges from their bottom anchorages and sent them drifting away in the grip of waves and winds. As the waters covered old cattail heads, submerged beaches, mudbanks and shores, the lodges were driven forward. Many contained muskrats trapped inside. They had been unable to fight through the debris of wrecked plunge holes, and now the lodges were disintegrating as they tossed in the roiled waters. Hundreds of lodges were wrecked against the northern shores of the marsh. Others came tumbling into the pond, many of them breaking up as they came and spilling captive muskrats into the dark water. Datra curled up in his hollow tree and tried to ignore the tumult outside.

Now, with the thaw so ferociously underway, all the old patterns of Datra's life were interrupted. He faced one of his great annual crises. The direction of his life for the rest of the year would be measured by his behavior in the days of the coming spring. As new warmth overturned life and rejuvenated it, he must once again meet the fierce challenge of defending his territory. His instincts and experience would be two of his strengths. His short temper, his extreme intolerance of other muskrats, and his savage readiness to fight set him apart from the others. Some muskrats did not contest the arrival of strangers. They allowed them to enter their lodges and slept with them and shared stored food with them. But Datra did not live like that.

Even at birth he was different from his brothers and sisters. He was the largest, the first to suckle, the first to leave the lodge, the winner of all the family fights, the most aggressive and energetic of the youngsters. One evening, when Datra was young, marauding muskrats entered the lodge in search of meat, and it was he who met them at the mouth of the corridor and drove them back down the plunge hole.

Once out of the family lodge, Datra fought his own father for a share of the paternal territory and drove the older muskrat back while his brothers and sisters were forced to migrate. In this way he quickly became master of enough territory to provide food for his growing bulk. Now the time had come for him to defend his place again.

When Datra returned from the north shore of the pond to his lodge, he found it gone. He dived to the muddy bottom, the current swirling around him, but he found nothing except some sticks jutting up from the mud. The force of the flood had been very great. He saw another muskrat swimming nearby and exploring the bottom for food. Datra plunged forward without hesitation. The two animals twirled in a flurry of motion and the intruder was bitten three times in the belly. He quickly fled and Datra let him go.

A crow came to the edge of the pond and walked with quick, jerky footsteps, hunting the shallows. On all sides of Datra the rest of the pond was awakening. Millions of tiny lives moved limbs that had been stiffened in sleep; millions of bleary eyes opened to see the sun of spring. Datra swam along a shore still patched with snow and yellowing ice. He saw groggy insects appear, heard the scurry of mice's feet kicking out new burrows in the wet earth. He nibbled at a newly-dead dragonfly larva, knowing he now faced a double challenge. He needed a new home and he must defend his territory. The blood flowed faster in his veins. He left his V-shaped water track behind him in aimless journeys across the pond. He slept in the hollow log, making no effort to rebuild his lodge. He fought sporadic battles with intruding muskrats from the marsh.

The winter had been a time of dull endurance, but now Datra was totally possessed by a new feeling. In the darkness of the hollow log he groomed himself thoroughly. He slipped out of the end of the log, scampered through the leaves and across the mud, and plunged into the pond. He surfaced cautiously and looked beyond the place where his lodge had been. The sun glinted on pieces of ice still remaining in sheltered places. Other muskrats sunned themselves on stones and among dead reeds. They were survivors of the flood and had come into the pond as prisoners in their floating lodges. Datra climbed up on a half-submerged branch, crouched down, and welcomed the warmth of the sun stealing into him. He felt his body tingling. He wanted to run and swim, all at once. But he knew that this was a time of movement for all muskrats, and so he sunned himself and remained the short-tempered guardian of his territory.

He saw them traveling in their cautious way, walking the edge of the pond, or swimming across it. He saw them haul themselves out of the water and walk carefully among the dry leaves of the forest. He saw one muskrat standing on an ice floe in a bay of the pond while the wind drove him out into the sun.

Datra's restlessness grew and he swam to the east, moving into the stream leading into the pond. Eventually, he came to the marsh, which exploded before his eyes in a confusing mixture of sights and sounds. The salamanders were moving and they seemed to have sprung in the thousands out of the earth itself, slipping past him on all sides. Their numbers brought out the great horned owl in daylight. Datra shivered at the sound of his booming, hollow cry. Then came the screams of outraged crows, the high cries of gulls, the quacking of ducks and the distant gabbling of geese, while nearby the marsh birds sang their own songs to the spring. Datra climbed on top of an old lodge and peered far across the marsh. Gray, scudding clouds moved behind speeding clots of ducks. A hawk hovered against the wind, and dancing wave caps ran through the wreckage of last summer.

Datra's restlessness had no direction. The marsh disturbed him with its great open spaces and its hordes of creatures. He quickly returned to the pond. There his mood changed again and he swam rapidly to the place where his great lodge had stood. Quick anger rose in him, a rage to defend this place against all comers, to possess it for himself alone. Not a single animal must be allowed to pass here. As he floated, his anger grew. A muskrat swam nearby and Datra drove him underwater and then chased him far across the pond.

Datra had resolved the boundaries of his territory for the new season, but an invasion of muskrats was beginning and he would have to fight for it. South and east of the pond, other muskrat populations were spreading out as the creatures sought to relieve the pressure of their numbers. A few of them appeared in the pond's outlet stream. They entered the pond and then stopped in consternation when Datra attacked furiously, darting from one intruder to another.

They fell back, retreating to pools lower down in the stream.

But fighting was not enough. Datra had to build, too. He moved along the pond's shores and ripped up dried debris and carried it in his mouth to the foundation of his new lodge. As he worked, the invaders came up the stream again and Datra dropped his building materials and fought them. A dozen animals swam together, but the ferocity of Datra's defense was so great that he turned them all back. After four days of fighting and building, more than a hundred muskrats were dammed up in the stream and the pressure to breach the defense of the pond became tremendous.

On the fifth day, when Datra had built the foundation of his lodge, nearly all the intruding muskrats began to move together. Their hurrying bodies filled the stream and they came into the pond in a mass. This time, Datra's most frantic efforts, his lunging attacks, his desperate swimming, could not stem the flood of migrants. While he bit the flank of one large male, six others passed by on either side of him. While he chased a female into the shallows, ten other muskrats swam behind him in deeper water. By midday, all was quiet. The muskrats had passed through the pond and gone onward to the uncertainties of the west.

Datra kept working, but he never hesitated to drop his load of dried reeds and fight. He knew that a fleeing muskrat was vulnerable. It was always better to turn and fight, even if the attacker were a fox or a mink.

While he was rummaging in the shallows for shards of dry

vegetation, a fox suddenly appeared a pace away. Datra quickly reared up and snapped his teeth. Instead of springing forward and killing him, as he might so easily have done, the fox hesitated and bared his teeth. Emboldened, Datra lunged forward and the fox drew back, cautious now at such unexpected hostility, turned, and trotted back into the trees.

One day when Datra was rooting among the debris of the wet woods for building material, he heard the quick rustle of an approaching body. He turned in time to see a mink, teeth bared, leaping at him. The attacking animal struck him near his throat, his sharp teeth penetrating Datra's skin and all but throwing him off his balance. But as the mink had attacked, Datra had reared up, his back falling against the trunk of a nearby tree. He kept his footing and wrenched the mink to one side. She attacked again and this time ran straight into Datra's large teeth, screaming when the teeth cut into her nose. The mink attacked again, but she could not throw Datra off his balance, so she turned and slipped away into the pond.

As Datra worked on his new lodge, the pond burgeoned with life. Migrant birds swept low over its water. Great collections of crows gathered noisily in high trees. Datra swam in cloudy water, through the new life flushing up from its depths. He passed yellow perch moving from deep hollows into the shallows where each female poured out long, jellied ribbons embedded with hundreds of eggs. He swam among spotted salamanders, their glistening black bodies richly touched with yellow, as they came down from the forest into the pond. When Datra swam into the shallows, he was among the male salamanders leaving spermatophores in the pond soon to be picked up by the females and held in their bodies until the eggs were laid. He watched skittering turtles swimming for food and saw sow bugs come into the pond from the eastern stream. They fed on rotting vegetation at the bottom, and the crayfish came out of their mud refuges and ate them. A bullfrog moved sluggishly up from the deepest part of the pond, passing Datra on his slow journey to the surface.

The roof of Datra's lodge bulked untidily above the waters of the pond. He fought less frequently now as the flow of muskrats from the east thinned to almost nothing and the other muskrats who had taken their places in the pond recognized his hold over his territory. Soon, while the broad, green spears of vegetation began rising from the shallows of the pond, Datra could enter his new lodge and climb, secure and dry, into its large, central resting chamber.

CHAPTER IV

The rough, rounded bulk of the new lodge looked like a small island in the pond. Datra climbed, dripping, up its side and began sunning himself on the roof. The lodge was a mark of his ownership of this territory. From it, he could look around on all sides and see who was trespassing, what was dangerous. But the new season was so rich with fresh life that his enemies were little interested in him now. He understood this, and allowed himself to doze in the sunlight without thought of mink or owl.

The pond was in a fever of activity. Its creatures went through many quick, colorful courtships and matings. Fighting crayfish wrenched off each others' claws, but they would grow back. Bisexual snails mated quietly in a group, each

43

snail playing both male and female roles simultaneously. Frogs gripped females tightly, their long embraces encouraging the development of the ripe eggs inside the females' bodies. When finally the eggs were ejected in jellied masses, the males released their sperm cells over the floating eggs and separated from their mates. Bird song rang from every tree. Foxes yapped and gulls screamed high in the sky. When Datra opened one eye, he saw that a female muskrat was not two bodies' lengths from him, rooting among some vegetation at the edge of his lodge. Datra watched her for a moment, then let himself down smoothly into the water where he remained still, his eyes fixed on her. She pretended not to notice him and continued her rooting. But when he moved closer, his nose almost touching her shoulder, she turned and swam off rapidly across the pond.

The thought of the female possessed Datra. He watched for her the rest of that day. On the following day, he met her in the middle of the pond. Again, she was alone. Again, he approached her, but this time more insistently. And again, she avoided him and tried to get away, but he swam behind her and now it was understood they would mate. She would not necessarily remain in his territory, or use his lodge to bear her young. She might go off to another part of the pond, or even into the marsh.

The female swam slowly and Datra easily overtook her, seizing her by the neck. The two animals fought a quick, mock battle, spinning in the water before the female fled again. Each mock fight made the female a little more excited. By mid-morning, the two animals had mated and were floating motionless, almost nose to nose, near Datra's lodge.

As always, Datra would have no single mate. He would prowl the limits of his territory, and sometimes beyond, attempting to mate with any female who attracted him. He knew he must fight with males who fancied the same female, but his size and strength usually meant victory.

The nights were busy times. He swam from one feeding platform to another, threading his way through islands of new vegetation, visiting favorite feeding places. Wherever the fancy took him, he sprayed some of his powerful, musky scent in these places. The scent was produced by two small glands and was profoundly important to all muskrats, particularly in the breeding season. Different scents identified individual animals. Some scents were signals, others warnings, still others invitations. The favorite spraying places were overlaid with one scent upon the other, each muskrat bound to try and make his own overpower all the others before him.

Now Datra swam among great masses of frog spawn, the jellied buffer protecting the eggs against drying, fungus attacks, and egg-hunters. He could see the dark sphere inside each egg which, beyond his range of vision, was dividing and re-dividing until groups of cells were formed. Soon, in the warm sun, the tadpoles would swim mouthless and limbless, free from the egg masses. But as yet they were too small for Datra to see the three pairs of protruding gills which were their life link to the water. He could not see the adhesive organs on their heads which fixed them to water weeds. There, groups of them hung together in rows. Soon their mouths would form and open, their gut coils would grow, and the tadpoles would begin to eat algae and the softest parts of water plants.

Through all this expansion of life, Datra moved in heedless haste, obsessed by his own pursuit of the season. He fought great and meaningless battles with other male muskrats, often for the privilege of mating with females who had long since swum away. But it was his duty, in this frantic time, to mate with as many females as possible.

Many of the animals at the pond were driven in this way. The act of procreation was unreasonable, astounding, miraculous. As the day died, millions of male mosquitoes rose in steep columns over the pond and marsh, and their expectant females rose to meet them. They were gripped by the males, and when the mating was completed, they were ready to lay their eggs.

Lumps were appearing on the bodies of the hydras, each new hydra sprouting its own tentacles and becoming a miniature reproduction of the adult. The bodies of the youngsters were hollow and led directly into the hollow body cavities of the adults. Together, both parents and youngsters seized passing worms, breaking them in two, the separate parts entering by separate mouths but ending in the common stomach at the base of the parent animal.

So enthusiastic was Datra's pursuit of female muskrats that he had little time to hunt. He seized his meals where he could, gobbling down roots and snails, and hastening on to his next chase. Sometimes his food came to him when others, even more absorbed than he, became his victims. He fought briefly with a female at the western end of the pond and was repulsed with vicious bites. He spun away in the water, bleeding from a wound in his flank, and accidentally blundered into a helpless female crayfish. She, like her lobster cousins in the sea, was lying on her back between the shelter of two stones. Her abdomen was curved upward and hundreds of eggs contained in a sticky matrix solution were flowing over it. The eggs stuck to her swimmerets, and if Datra had not collided with her, the young crayfish would have begun to hatch in seven days. Instead, Datra seized her and ate her.

This was a time of life and a time of death and both moved in hidden ways. When Datra swam along the bottom of the pond, a large turtle came gracefully through the water above him, heading toward his lodge. Datra turned and followed. He saw the turtle haul himself up on a nearby mudbank and reach the platform where some of the muskrats usually dragged their food to eat. Datra surfaced nearby and watched while the turtle ate five naked, new-born muskrats who had been left there by their mother to die. She had taken with her only those youngsters whom she could rear inside the lodge. The others had to be sacrificed to the pond.

When Datra surfaced in the pond, he saw other creatures caught up in the tumult of the spring. The redwings, feathers inflated, were everywhere. The males gurgled and chuckled and puffed out their chests, the scarlet patches of their wing feathers snapping across the pond like beacons, the first hot color of the new season. A pair of butterflies trembled on a leaf, their bodies arched in mating frenzy. A warbler took tiny steps along a branch with his body stretched into the shape of a tear drop and his wings fluttering. Suddenly, he flew at the female who awaited him and balanced himself on her back. The female flicked her tail and the male thrust down. A crow, feathers fluffed out, danced his courtship in a high tree. In the greening branches, birds chased each other in mad flights. The jagged cry of the meadow lark sounded.

In the pond itself, as the push of vegetation grew around him, Datra swam among an outpouring of tiny lives. A dragonfly nymph pulsed water from her abdomen to power herself forward toward a water plantain stem. She began to climb the stem, still breathing in water and expelling it after extracting its vital oxygen. But inside her tough skin, the dragonfly's adult body was preparing to emerge. She climbed up the stem and out of the water and waited in the sun while her nymph skin dried and split up the back, releasing a slimy creature with wet wings plastered to its body.

Datra hastened on. He chased a female into a tangle of plants and lost her. His passage dislodged the hard, brown empty shell of the dragonfly nymph which had been fastened to the plantain stem. He saw a lean, yellow-footed hawk standing on a branch near the shores of the pond. Long ago, a pair of these hawks had come to the pond and terrorized its birds. They had flashed round its shores, chasing redwings and robins, woodpeckers and sparrows. As Datra watched now, the hawk bolted from its branch and came speeding across the pond. Datra dived. He came to the surface with his eyes just above the water level among some swelling reeds and saw two of these hawks fighting with a pair of crows for possession of a tree.

New plants grew all around Datra's lodge. Some pierced the foundations of his building. They grew in groups and expanded, pushing against other groups nearby, all competing for a share of air and water and sunlight.

Datra swam among great tangles of bulrush roots, packed so densely together that no other competitor could get among them. The root tangles moved gradually away from the shore of the pond, picking up mud and giving Datra footholds to draw himself out of the water and prowl among their rustling leaves. The bulrush platforms would one day fill the pond if they were allowed to expand without interruption.

But just as Datra was vulnerable to the changing seasons, so were the bulrushes. Their effort to expand was so great that the hearts of their territories became weak. Other plants got in among them, fought them for a share of the room, and so suppressed their growth. Soon, the hearts of the bulrush communities would begin to die out.

The excitement of the new season was evident in all life forms and no animal or plant in the pond enjoyed relief from the constant struggle to dominate over all others. The cattails were nearly as dense as the bulrushes and were building up almost solid soil from the quaking mud of the pond shores. But they were as vulnerable as the bulrushes. Their work created ideal places for the sedges which, in time, would strangle the cattails. Then the coarse plants would take over the work of trying to transform Datra's pond into dry land.

Every part of Datra's body was charged with the thrill of the chase, the fight, the conquest. Underwater, he reigned supreme. Recently, no other creature seriously contested his

rights. But one morning, Datra panicked. He was chasing an intruding muskrat when the water ahead suddenly moved with the passage of a great body. An otter, a lithe and graceful water creature, flashed past Datra toward the center of the pond.

Datra remembered otters the way he remembered small hawks. When he was very young, they had come to the pond. In a few days, the otters had destroyed its many intricate balances of life. They had wrecked the muskrat lodges. They sent the frogs and turtles burrowing for safety in the deepest mud. They roiled the water so that it became cloudy and impossible to see through.

Now Datra turned away from his chase and apprehensively circled back toward his lodge. But before he came within range of that familiar place, the otter appeared again. This time he made directly for Datra. With a powerful flick of his tail, and with his strong back legs working hard, Datra

thrust himself down, heading for the bottom. He felt the pressure of the water change as the big otter surged overhead. Datra could find no proper refuge in the bottom. He half-kicked, half-clawed his way through mud and debris, churning the water behind him in a kind of submarine smoke screen. The otter passed again, now invisible. Datra forced himself forward. The water became shallower and Datra appeared out of the mud he had kicked up. With no hope of turning back, Datra hurled himself into the muddy bottom and dug madly. The otter arrived at the spot where Datra had disappeared, but was driven back, blinded by a jet of mud kicked from Datra's powerful digging. The otter remained, curious and inquisitive, listening to the sounds of Datra's digging. But he soon turned away and swam off.

Datra had no way of knowing that the otter had gone. He continued to dig, creating a long, curving path which took him out of the mud and into the soil of the shore. Exhausted, he paused for a moment in the pitch blackness before digging again. He burst into view among tangled grasses at the edge of the pond. Clouds moved overhead. Birds sang. The pond whispered. Of the otter, there was no sign.

Datra was so badly frightened that he could not even look at the pond. He turned and loped through the shrubs. As long as he was in panic, there could be no turning back. Blindly he raced on, skirting trees, kicking up leaves, oblivious to the spectacle he was making in the quiet woods. Then, panting, he reached the wet land at the edge of the marsh. Thankfully he ran through its shallows, plunged and swam deeper.

Almost immediately, Datra came to another muskrat lodge. In the dim light of the green water, tendrils of rubbish hung down from the floating base of the lodge. Datra swam through these into the dark shadows directly under the house. Above him were two gaping, pitch-black holes. He hesitated, but after a moment he swam up one.

Climbing to the top of the tunnel, he entered the main living chamber of the biggest lodge he had ever seen. His panic subsided as he set out to explore this many-roomed home. Three tunnels led from the main room to other rooms. One led upward in a curve to another, smaller chamber almost directly above the main room. This, the smell indicated, was the place where suckling young were reared. As Datra worked his way cautiously in the darkness from one room to another, he found living chambers and birth chambers, rooms for transient muskrats and storage rooms for food. A score or more of muskrats must have occupied this lodge.

The absence of animals distressed Datra. It was unnatural and uncanny. The smell of the animals lingered in the corridors. Whatever disaster had befallen this great house, it had been complete and recent. There was no living thing left in the lodge.

It took Datra three days to return to the pond, three days of agony as he made many attempts to go home. Each time, as he worked his way into the shallowing water, some danger signal sent him back to the security of the great lodge. Eventually he made the journey at night, a time that was just as frightening as the day. His journey was interrupted twice by a raccoon who inquisitively followed his scent for a few minutes. And when, in darkness, the moon wobbling uncertainly over the rippling waters of the pond, he swam into his lodge, he found it was occupied by strangers.

CHAPTER V

The muskrats who had moved into Datra's lodge were ready to fight. Datra's territory had become their territory. His lodge had become theirs. In his absence, other muskrats had come to the pond and territories were cramped. When Datra paused, just out of the water of his main plunge hole, he sniffed the air for a long time before moving again. His own feeling for his territory was not as strong as before. He was less ready to fight for it than he had been a few days earlier. As he moved up into the lodge, he was prepared to compromise with the creatures living in it.

But he was given no chance. A shape hurled itself down out of the darkness and struck him head-on. This was a male muskrat who had occupied the lodge two days before and had taken Datra's territory. Now he was determined to defend it.

The attack galvanized Datra. This was *his* lodge, *his* place. He seized the intruder, turned him over quickly inside the corridor, and shoved him deep underwater, holding him there firmly while the desperate animal struggled, scrabbling the walls and ceiling in his effort to escape. Datra did not mean to kill the intruder, but he had made a tight grip on the other animal's throat before he had had a chance to take a breath. His struggles ceased as Datra dragged him down the corridor. Datra released the body and turned back toward the center of the lodge. He entered the main chamber and found it empty. He moved toward two secondary rooms, smelling other muskrats. When he entered the first room, he was ready to fight. But he found only a young, inexperienced muskrat who had followed the other, older animal when he had occupied the lodge. Datra ignored his chattering teeth, grabbed him by the back of the neck, and dragged him out of the lodge. The youngster was terrified and Datra pulled him well clear of the lodge before he released him with two punishing bites.

As Datra swam up his main plunge hole, he found the body of the first muskrat blocking his way. He pulled him out of the hole, and returned to the lodge. In the second food-storage chamber, he found a female. Datra entered, his teeth chattering in readiness for a fight, but his rage was softened by the sex of the other animal. He moved forward, as if to seize her, but paused an inch from her body. The female ignored him. She was readying herself to give birth to young.

Datra still wanted to clear his lodge, but he found it impossible to move against this creature. He reached forward, gripped, and pulled. She resisted him. He drew back a little, puzzled by his conflict of feelings. After a while, he withdrew. Behind him, young muskrats were being born.

Over the next few days, a change occurred among the muskrats of Datra's world. They had been living in harmony; their numbers were in balance. But now, a new and sinister force spread through the marsh and entered the pond. Datra felt the urge. It seemed to grip his limbs, impelling him forward. He left the central chamber and went to the female's room. Inside, young muskrats whimpered with hunger. Their mother was in the pond, hunting. Suddenly determined, Datra bent down to bite one of the youngsters, the urge to kill so strong inside him that he wanted to destroy this family.

But the desire to kill was matched by another urge—his feeling for life itself. And so he waited, trembling. He licked his paws to get rid of the feeling. He bent down again to bite, to kill, but the other urge, to preserve and save, came on strongly. Then, unable to master either of the desires, he turned and scuttled from the lodge.

Elsewhere, other muskrats were not so indecisive. Too many youngsters were being born, it seemed, and the surplus young must be killed. In lodge after lodge adult muskrats entered and murdered the youngsters. Terrible fights occurred in corridors when females defended their litters and struggled with stronger, killer males. Muskrats reeled from the lodges, their bodies streaming blood, as both mothers and intruders died in their efforts to kill and to preserve life.

As abruptly as it had started, the killing stopped. The murderous feeling disappeared, to remain dormant until it was needed again. Datra came hesitantly into the female's room, but he was driven back by her snapping teeth. Now, he was merely inquisitive. His urge to kill, to destroy, had left him completely.

He reveled in the pulsing pond, basked in the warm sun, felt life pulsing all around him. He ate the plants of the pond and did not know that he was dependant on billions of invisible plants swirling around him every time he swam through the water. The desmids and the diatoms were the genesis of all life in the pond. These single-celled plants grew in a variety of beautiful forms. The desmids thrived in the fresh, sweet water at the western end of the pond where they sought the sun and warmth, sticking themselves to the stems of larger plants in fine, green films, or hiding among the leaves of other aquatic vegetation. Each was invisible by itself, but when packed together, they could be seen. Their bodies were stuffed with greenish chlorophyll, their surfaces smooth, finely marked, or roughened by spines or dents. They could dig themselves free from burial in the mud and work their way through the pond's waters to share in its life.

In the shallows, where the water was not so fresh, the diatoms thrived. They were as impatient and as active as the desmids, with microscopic shells made of nearly pure silica, and they were so tiny that one hundred million of them would not fill Datra's stomach.

Sometimes, when the sun was bright and Datra was swimming slowly, he saw specks of life in the water. These were the tiny plant-eaters who hunted for the diatoms and desmids. The amoebae reached out part of their jellied substance until their victims were drawn into the centers of their bloblike bodies and digested.

More visible, more fierce, more direct were the hydras which he could see stuck like fine hairs to the stems of plants. Their bodies reached out in a continual search for water fleas, tiny worms or microscopic pieces of meat torn from the bodies of victims killed in other struggles. Datra brushed past these tiny killers, unconcerned that these efficient hunters fired poisonous stings into their victims.

The pond was filled with hunters working at every level of existence. When a fly fell into the water, tiny water moles gathered around its body and fastened to it a cloudy fringe of filaments. Each filament contained a sporangia which would later rupture and release free-swimming spores that would go in search of new corpses. Bristle-bodied aquatic worms, prowling the ooze, fed on material already decaying. Some bred by dividing in the middle while others laid eggs.

As the pond matured, the bryozoans spread over weeds, stones, and on fallen branches. They were moss-like in their tightly packed colonies, thousands of animals together, each with raised cilia which moved water and food into their mouths. They were like a living skin on many of the pond's parts, at an odd distance between plant and animal, and their success blurred the difference between the two.

The growth of the water flea populations, visible to Datra now, transformed the pond. The fleas were the basic food source for nearly all the creatures in the pond and they spread prosperity wherever they thrived. But their enormous demands for food quickly eliminated all that was available to them, and they rapidly changed their behavior. Eggs miraculously produced males, instead of continual generations of females. These hatched quickly and the new creatures mated with the existing females. Their fertilized eggs were quite different from the earlier ones. They were larger and yolkier, with thick, hard shells designed to help them last through the hard times of winter when they would lie dormant until spring arrived. These eggs would sink to the bottom of the pond and remain there during the fall and winter until they hatched and triggered the female generations again. It was possible for them to receive a signal in late summer that times were good again, in which case they would spring to life, producing new generations of female water fleas before winter closed the pond in sleep.

One night, with warm air flooding in from the south, with moisture dripping from the trees, and with the moon trying to shine through wet, fleecy clouds, the frogs made their uproar. They squeaked and groaned and yipped and grunted and growled. Frogs stood on leaves, in mud, awash in the water around Datra, and even in the tallest trees. They roared out their praise to this exciting season. But the voice of the pond was sensitive to intrusion. It could be stilled in a second. Datra dived off his lodge and the slap of his body hitting the water produced an instant silence. A change in the weather could still the pond's voice. On the following night, the rush of warm air ended and brief, quick cold poured in from the north. The pond was utterly silent. Datra surfaced to the sound of the hiss and chatter of falling water, but no voice cried out.

For all the creatures, it was a time of movement and change. Datra swam east the full length of the pond into its broad, warm shallows, and headed for the marsh. The journey expressed his own restlessness, not his need to hunt there. A fox, muzzle yearning forward, followed his passage from the shores of the stream. The fox dropped behind and Datra reached the marsh, scuttled through undergrowth and young willow trees, and splashed out into its shallows.

As he swam along now, his whiskered nose just above the water, an uproar of crow voices approached. He ducked underwater with a powerful swirl of his tail and struck bottom immediately. He swam off quickly, zigzagging back and forth until he found cover in some debris collected near the shore and burrowed into it. The crow voices were loud and near and harrying. The smell of death hung in the water. He returned quickly to the less dangerous waters of the pond.

But even at the pond, nothing was ever predictable. A new crisis came. Strange populations of muskrats invaded his waters from the woodlands to the north. Datra found himself fighting again, but the fighting was exhausting, and the numbers of muskrats overwhelming. He withdrew into his lodge and fought only when others attempted to enter it.

The arrival of these muskrat legions brought other hunters with them. The minks made the pond their hunting ground, taking over muskrat lodges after they had murdered the inhabitants. More raccoons came into Datra's territory. He saw them at dusk, prowling the shores as they looked out hopefully for signs of muskrats in distress. The great horned owl came to the pond by day and night, drifting through the northern trees and arriving with a splay of wings. He took muskrats, dripping from the water, or sent them spinning from the tops of their lodges.

Now Datra could not go to the marsh. The pressure of numbers there was so great that fighting was constant. A parade of beaten muskrats began passing through the pond, losers in the fight for space and survival in the marsh.

Datra watched their progress with mounting concern. He saw one muskrat, blinded in a fight, blunder across the pond into the jaws of a waiting fox. Raccoons splashed into the water at dusk and caught muskrats in sudden flurries of action, dragging them away to the shore. Datra came across one animal struggling in the pond shallows, his long tail flailing and his entrails caught in a mass of pond weeds.

The fighting sapped the determination and the will to live of those surviving. In this terrible time, Datra returned to his lodge to find a muskrat at its entrance. He surged forward to fight. But the other animal, already beaten in many other battles, turned his back and put his head down submissively. He refused to respond to Datra's lunges, his challenges to fight. Datra paused, confused, but then he recognized the other's submission. There was no need to fight or to kill. Instead, he gripped the intruder by the neck and dragged him away from the lodge until he reached the out-going current. There he released the intruder, who floated away, apathetic and submissive, and disappeared.

Every creature at the pond paid a price for imbalances in their numbers. The insects felt this pressure and so did solitary bears. A chorus of yapping foxes encircled the pond. They, too, were in crisis, victims of an epidemic of rabies. The deadly disease moved from fox to fox and made them mad. They charged through the forest, some of them hurling themselves into the pond in their frenzy, thrashing about and attempting to bite anything that came within reach. They bit their comrades and infected them. They snarled and yapped without cause. And then, finally, lethargy seized them. Jaws became paralyzed, limbs stiffened, and death ended their misery.

Now a new mood strengthened the muskrats who had been forced from the marsh. They were no longer beaten animals, but aggressive, ready to fight hard to regain lost homes and territories. They pressed in on Datra. He fought them, but there were far too many, and the pond became an arena for their battles. The gouges and rips on Datra's hide never had a chance to heal. His ears were tattered and often white bone showed on his legs from the slash marks suffered in fierce fights.

Through all this bloody turmoil, new generations of musk-rats kept thrusting forward, adding their demands to those of the older animals.

Datra felt his strength ebbing. He drove off two intruders, but he knew he was scarcely able to fight again. He swam slowly in search of food. Then, coming steadily at him, he saw the largest muskrat in his experience. He was as large as Datra himself and his hide, too, was scarred, but his eyes were bright. The strokes of his limbs were powerful and determined. Datra, in panic, felt submission stealing through his bones. He had an overpowering urge to put his head down and admit defeat. The awful feeling gripped Datra and suddenly the large muskrat attacked.

CHAPTER VI

Datra cringed from his attacker, half-turning to one side so that his flank was exposed. His feeling of submission was now so strong that he could not even see the other muskrat. His eyes were open but they registered only a gray pall. He felt no pain, and so did not know that his enemy had chopped a deep wound into his flank. The force of the blow was so strong that Datra flipped upside down, his long back legs flailing out of the water. He gulped air, then water, choked, spat, sneezed. The gray pall lifted suddenly; his feeling of submission snapped, replaced by a flush of anger.

He twisted his body savagely to face his attacker, but there was nothing in the bloody water. He twirled again, just in time to meet a second attack. His enemy's great mouth was wide open and the flaring yellow teeth were parted, ready to take another bite. Datra ducked his head underwater, remembering an old trick. He half-rolled underwater and came up underneath the other muskrat. He felt his teeth sink deeply into his belly and hold, and he kept his grip as he was turned roughly in the water by the desperate efforts of the other animal to escape. Round and round Datra went, but with slowing speed, and when the rolling stopped, he slowly released his grip. The other muskrat floated in the water with his legs spread. The only sign of life was his sharp black eyes looking upward. His blood joined Datra's in the reddened water.

All muskrats could take fearful injuries in fights and yet not die. They could lose their tails and legs, or have a vital organ ripped, and survive. They were warriors, ready to fight at the first imagined trespass, and all the veterans of these muskrat wars displayed an unbelievable assortment of body scars. Datra's enemy would not die, but he would not stay in the pond either. Gradually he turned in a swirl of water, turning again and again until he was in the grip of the outward-going current. And then, still turning, he disappeared from Datra's sight.

Datra swam slowly back to his lodge, the wound in his flank throbbing each time he pumped his legs. He crawled into the lodge and lay panting on his bed. When the shock had passed somewhat, he licked the wound clean, knowing he must stay in the safety of the lodge until the injury closed.

The life of the pond came and went like the ebb and flow

of a tide. Surplus muskrats disappeared and were gone forever from pond and marsh, but in their places came hordes of young, now leaving lodges everywhere. The youngsters faced the same problem as did all the other surplus creatures. Datra had no family bond, and so he did not know how often he met his own youngsters as they searched for a place in the pond. When his wound had healed, he chivvied them relentlessly. He drove one young animal ashore where he, larger than any other youngster Datra had seen, turned on his father and fought him hard for a moment or two before turning and running off. Datra's character and courage and strength lived on in his oldest son of this season.

All around Datra, other young creatures were appearing at the pond. Birds fell from nests, urging their clumsy bodies across the waters of the pond. Some fell in. Some made unsteady landings on the farther shore. One day, standing on top of his lodge, he heard a distant uproar of crow cries and did not know this meant that a nest of young crows was ready to leave. He did see the lean, yellow-footed hawks perched in a tree near the pond. They still frightened him when they made their fast flights overhead; and when one of them appeared abruptly on a branch near his lodge, he slipped down into the water, turned, and left just his cautious snout showing.

At that moment a young crow bolted from a nest to the east of the pond and glided toward Datra. He saw the big bird falling toward the pond, wings outspread, still uncertain how to fly. As he got control of his wings, flattened out, and began an unsteady thrashing toward the southern shore,

the hawk leaped from his perch. Datra dived immediately, assuming the attack was against him.

Deep in the waters of the pond, pulsing forward away from his lodge, he did not see the explosion of feathers when the hawk hit the young crow. But he heard the thud of the crow hitting the water, and saw the young bird's agonized wings splayed out in silhouette against the sun.

The crow had fallen heavily and was dying, but the hawk had hit it with such power that his claws were still fastened into the crow's body, and he was borne down in the fall of the young bird. Datra saw his lean, lithe body struggling,

trying to get his head above water. But his struggles were
weak. He had broken one of his wings in the attack. As
Datra watched, the hawk regained the surface, withdrew
his claws, and left the dead crow behind. He slapped clumsily away toward the shore. He would go off into the woods
and die there because he was unable to hunt.

Datra remained on the bottom, still motionless, still watch-
ing warily. Then he allowed himself to float upward until he
reached the body of the crow. He took one of the crow's feet
between his two large front teeth and pulled tentatively. But
the body was big and the mass of black feathers blossomed
so wide in the water that Datra was intimidated. He turned
away and swam back to his lodge.

A raccoon came to the shores of the pond, waded into its
shallows in the dusk, and reached down into the mud. Behind her, a group of young raccoons watched their mother.

Datra remained motionless in green vegetation and heard the squelching of mud being squeezed through her paws, the rustle of water as she washed mud off a snail, the crack of the shell being broken, and the chewing of her jaws as she ate.

Datra was afraid of the raccoon. She roamed the pond day and night. He knew that she favored the cattail jungles and hunted through them so regularly that she had made her own paths in the thickets. Sometimes Datra used them himself, although he mistrusted the powerful raccoon scent of the other creature. She was huge compared with himself, and when he met her on these paths, he would stop in terror, standing up and chattering his teeth in a futile attempt to intimidate her. Usually she showed no interest in him and turned away, but once she had stood up too, and the sight of this immense animal towering above him so unnerved Datra that he scuttled off at full speed.

Datra watched the raccoon from the seclusion of the water-logged roots of the cattails. He watched her moving through the soft green daylight, her intent black eyes looking all about her as she stopped to pick a dragonfly nymph from the stem of a plant. She peeled off its hard outer skin before eating it. The raccoon did not seem dangerous now, but Datra knew she was an enemy. His memories were too sharp of groups of raccoons tearing muskrat lodges to pieces, pulling out the youngsters from their homes, killing and eating everything they could find. He remained wary of this raccoon, although she paid no attention to him.

The young muskrats of the pond faced a hard choice:

fight or be driven off. Usually they were easy to intimidate. Datra's great size and determination often sent them off without a fight. But his eldest son of this season, with a deadly kind of determination, challenged Datra inside his own lodge. Datra was dozing in his main lodge room when he heard the youngster moving cautiously up the corridor to his room. Immediately he dashed down the corridor and hurled himself at the intruder.

But instead of the usual perfunctory struggle, a few slashes of teeth, and flight, this young muskrat attacked. Datra was bitten four times in the face, and was so shocked that he momentarily retreated. The young intruder came at him again. But now Datra was murderously angry and he attacked with such ferocity that the intruder was hurled back. When he tried to turn in the narrow corridor, the enraged Datra bit him severely along his flanks. He fled from his father's rage.

All through the pond, the fight for life was just as impersonal, just as decisive. When Datra swam along the bottom, he encountered thousands of minnows who were being eaten by bass and pickerel, kingfisher and mink, dragonfly nymph and heron. Datra darted among their flickering bodies and caught a slow fish himself.

The minnows were decimated, a thousand of them dying in one day. The slaughter continued until only the fittest, or the luckiest, survived, skulking in the long weeds of the shallows. Only a few hundred would live through the summer to endure the hard winter of the pond.

The scavengers feasted as the bloody contest between

hunter and hunted was played out. Thousands of small crustaceans explored the bottom of the pond, looking for the remains of shredded bodies forgotten by the hunters. Young leeches clung to their mothers, who tried to protect them with blood-sucking bites from predatory fish. The eggs hatched on a male great diving beetle's back (where the female had cemented them for safekeeping), and the first youngster free from the egg case turned and began to eat his beetle brothers.

Clam eggs hatched into tiny, shelled replicas of the adults. They fastened themselves to fish in order to make the trip to their permanent homes. There they sank into the mud to begin their precarious new lives. Young turtles moved toward the pond, but their shells were still soft and not many survived the dangerous journey. The young spilled into the pond, where their chances of survival were small. Newborn insects tested their untried wings and fell by the thousands into the pond, where they were eaten by fish and other insects.

Datra swam in this abundance of food, and it would have been his best time were it not for the son whom he had vanquished inside his lodge. The youngster, so large and so persistent, seemed fascinated by Datra's territory, and he prowled its edges constantly, making darting forays into it to hunt or to harry Datra as he went about his own business. There was no law of the pond that said the young muskrat must, or must not, have this territory. The law said only that the two animals must fight for its possession. One year, sometime, somewhere, Datra would meet a muskrat like this one and find his power and determination mastered by something stronger. Then he would be driven off to become a nomad searching for safety.

As he lay on top of his lodge in the bright, early morning sun, his body camouflaged against the dried rubbish of the lodge roof, Datra heard a sudden sound and found himself seized by his haunches in a powerful grip. Then, with a painful jerk, he was dragged off the lodge root and deep down into the water. He struggled frantically but could not break that deadly grip.

CHAPTER VII

The grip on Datra's thigh was
so tight that he could not turn to get his teeth into his enemy.
He could not even see who had attacked him. The grip pre-
vented him from using his powerful back legs to twist himself around or to kick himself free. Down he went, deep into
the jungle of plants streaming up from the muddy bottom,
finding himself pushed headfirst into the black muck. For
one tiny moment, as his nose dug into the mud, the terrible
grip relaxed. Datra twisted himself free. And now he saw
the other muskrat. He was his great enemy of the season,
his firstborn son of this year.

But blood meant nothing. The two animals closed in on
one another without hesitation. Long teeth sliced like daggers.

The mud whirled up in dense, streaming clouds which soon obscured both animals. Datra's rage, which had been rising through the previous fights, was now so great that when he got a throat grip on his son, he held on grimly.

Both muskrats were soon short of air, but their passion was so intense that neither was prepared to break off. Datra felt his lungs heave, but he held on, tightening his grip. Still the other muskrat struggled. Pinpoints of light appeared in the darkened water before Datra's eyes. Slowly, almost reluctantly, the two of them floated up out of the cloud of mud, both bodies now still. Their sleek backs broke the surface waters of the pond and Datra immediately released his grip and took one shuddering breath into his lungs.

The other muskrat remained still for a long moment, his head below the surface, his eyes open, the water turning pink around him. Then he, too, lifted his head and drew in a rasping breath, blood dripping from his lacerated throat. Datra, seeing his enemy still alive, would have rushed forward to finish the fight, but he was too weak. Instead, he kicked feebly once, and then was still again, his flanks heaving with his fast breathing. When he looked back, he saw the other muskrat moving slowly away across the pond to the east. He had disappeared before Datra reached his lodge.

It was high summer, a time of unparalleled richness in the pond. All its creatures now reached the many fruitions of their individual lives. Datra lay three-parts submerged in water that was green with life all around him. Lily pads jostled. Soft breezes touched the water, and dragonflies hawked low overhead. The great frog chorus of spring was over. The water everywhere rippled with the movements of young frogs testing their new legs. The hot sun burned down directly among the still trees. Perfect peace and contentment enfolded the pond and Datra floated happily in its embrace.

But the ways of the pond were never predictable for long. One day Datra watched a muskrat climb up on top of a half-sunken log where he usually sunned himself. The next day he saw him feebly attempting to climb the slippery sides of the log. He failed. He lay in the water, his nose and front feet up against the log, his back legs kicking. The following day the muskrat was dead. He floated against Datra's lodge, his body bobbing in tiny waves.

The epidemic became a plague and felled the muskrats with terrible swiftness. Datra saw muskrats he knew well become stricken one day, struggle against the bleeding sickness the next day, and die the third. The plague made all the muskrats edgy, almost hysterical. Datra left his lodge and was attacked immediately by a strange muskrat for no apparent reason. The fight was fierce and bitter, but the other muskrat unexpectedly broke away and fled. Datra himself felt restless. He found himself unaccountably attacking others, snapping his long teeth in contests over food, even though there was plenty of it.

The intensity of the plague wore down the muskrats so that they had little energy left to hunt for food. Every creature found himself pressed against the edge of death. In the marsh thousands of them sickened and died. Datra swam down his favorite channel toward the cattail roots and saw dead muskrats floating in the sun-splashed water above him. He saw dead muskrats lying on the bottom of the channel, eyes and jaws opened wide in the last pain of their disease.

Datra moved among stricken muskrats along the shores of his territory, and grew more uneasy every day. The disease tore at the guts of the muskrats and they bled from their mouths. Datra vaguely remembered another such disaster many years before, when he was very young. The water and the reeds had been teeming with muskrats before the epidemic hit. A scant thirty days later, he had swum the length and breadth of his territory looking in vain for other muskrats. Not until the spring of the next year had the pond been repopulated with migrant muskrats.

Datra himself finally contracted the disease. He felt it come on him in the late afternoon. His eyes clouded slightly. At first he thought twilight had come, but then, when he looked out toward the farther end of the pond, he saw neither darkness nor light, but a gray pall. Then stabbing pains seized his gut and back legs. He swam with difficulty along the channel back to his lodge. By the time he reached its submarine entrance, he scarcely had the strength to pull himself up into the chamber. All during that night the pains grew throughout his body. His head rang with the sound of thunder, and he moaned and whimpered.

But he was still alive on the following morning, although barely able to move. The hammering in his head went on relentlessly and his belly swelled. Weakly he tried to groom himself, but even the effort of licking his front paws was too much and he subsided with a gasp. At midday he stirred. He could not tell whether he had been asleep and dreaming or awake and seeing a procession of images. But now he could hear something digging into the outside wall of the lodge. Despite his sickness, he recognized the sound. It was a mink, quick and furtive, and digging hard. If the mink got into his lodge, he could not hope to plunge to safety. Slowly his fuddled brain understood all this. The mink. He thought of terrible injuries, of pain, of terror in the night. These thoughts helped to clear his brain, and his brain asked his body for one last rush of energy.

Groggily he got up, leaned against the wall of the lodge chamber, and gasped. The digging sounds quickened as the mink, hearing his moans, hastened forward. At the same time, Datra's awareness of the danger sharpened. Blood flowed faster through his body, making it tingle. He shook his head to dispel its dizziness, and turned toward the sound of digging. All was darkness. His first sight of the approaching enemy was a gradual lightening. Datra faced this light, breathing hard with his effort to be alert, to be strong, to be ready to fight. For a moment all was silent as the mink, now close enough to scent Datra, sniffed and peered forward. She heard Datra's breathing and the digging started again, faster now.

When the mink broke through the wall, Datra was so excited that he actually leaped forward. He misjudged the jump and struck the ceiling rather than leaping through the hole. His heart pounded. The mink, uncertain of what had happened in the gloom, paused. She was half-framed in the hole she had made and blocked the light from outside. Datra could not stop himself now. He chewed and slashed at the small hole, and the ferocity of his effort was so great that the mink drew back.

But the effort suddenly became too much for Datra. He felt his strength drain away from him like blood running from a wound. With his head halfway through the hole, he slumped down, panting. The mink reached forward and grabbed him by the skin of his neck and dragged his limp body out of the lodge. Another sharp-faced mink waited there, standing on top of the lodge, head raised, scenting the helpless muskrat. Datra, eyes bleared now from his abrupt collapse, saw the trees overhead turning upside down and sideways, his body rolling helplessly over as he was dragged to the roof of the lodge. He was so limp that the mink thought he was dead. Now she would tow his body to her cache of other victims stored in her den.

But Datra was not finished. Slower this time, but more certainly, his body was charging itself for another effort. He had not given up. He had not accepted the muskrat fate. Indeed, a rage to live, to survive and not accept the dominion of the mink, was growing again. He remained limp though, bumping over the dried reeds on top of the lodge, waiting for that moment when he might make his supreme, and perhaps final, effort.

The mink, all her attention concentrated on dragging

Datra's heavy body, a weight greater than her own, did not notice the slight stiffening in Datra's neck muscles. She had no experience of dead prey coming to life. And so she was caught unprepared when Datra, with a twist of his body, splayed his feet, braced his body, and then violently jerked his head upward. The move was made so quickly that the mink was thrown to one side and Datra was trimphantly upright, his long teeth protruding, his eyes bright again. The mink recovered and dashed forward, not believing what had happened. Her cheek was laid open to the bone by Datra's lunge. She drew back, bleeding. The second mink rushed forward and grabbed Datra from behind, and he fell, but again his teeth bit home. The second mink screamed and jerked himself away.

The first mink attacked again, despite her injury. She was still unable to believe in Datra's recovery. She slashed Datra's flank before he could get his teeth embedded in her back. Both animals turned double somersaults, momentarily locked together, and collided with the second mink. Surprised, he bit wildly but slashed the female instead of Datra.

By now Datra was bleeding from all his wounds, but his strength remained manic, his breathing a great rasping roar in his lungs. He attacked again and closed in on the second mink. His teeth struck twice and the mink dived into the pond to escape. He turned back to the first mink, who looked at him, eyes bright and inquiring, blood glistening on her fur. Recognizing Datra's determination, she too dived into the pond and disappeared.

Datra, the undefeated monarch of the pond at this moment, began to feel the fight. Blood roared in his head. Fiery pains shot through his body. He knew he had to reach shelter. He turned and half-dragged himself down the side of his lodge, quite forgetting the new entrance made by the mink. He readied himself to dive, but the effort was futile. The pond seemed to turn, first one way, then the other, and he slumped down, all the strength gone from his limbs. The world turned around twice and he lost consciousness.

CHAPTER VIII

The pond was still. The summer air had thickened, hot but kind, and the pond breathed its warmth. As the heat intensified, reaching into the deepest parts of the pond, thousands of creatures left its waters. Young mosquitoes struggled free from their pupating cases, which floated on the still water. As new adults, they stretched their wings to dry in the sun before flying off to find their first meal. The males would be content to drink the cool juice of plants, but the females would need the hot blood of animals and birds. Water beetles came to the surface, unfolded their wings, and flew. Other beetles arrived at the pond, folded air under their wings, and dived. In the pond, they would breathe this stored air. The pond shrank as its water evaporated in the heat. Newly created shallows spread, choking with aquatic plants where thousands of refugee young fish and minnows sought dubious safety.

In his lodge Datra slept a sleep that seemed close to death. It was a sleep of recovery, a sleep of repair, a sleep to forget. As he lay there, day after day, inert and scarcely breathing, his body systematically repaired the grievous damage of epidemic and bloody fight. In his dreams he relived those last terrible moments when the pond had turned over on top of him and sent him tumbling down into a great pit of darkness. He relived his awakening, the hot sun burning his wounds, his almost blind, step-by-step passage back into the lodge.

He lay near death, but with that stubborn tenacity typical of the muskrat, he would survive his terrible ordeal so long as his will to live was not impaired. He was very lucky. Nothing would have saved him had not a prowling fox walked gingerly out through the pond shallows to investigate the lodge and trodden down the walls, collapsing the hole dug by the mink. If the passage had not been blocked, Datra almost certainly would have been killed by marauding mink or died from the attentions of insects seeking to lay their eggs in his wounds.

Finally, days after the fight, he dragged himself down to his submarine tunnel, launched himself into the warm water, and swam deep and slowly to the bottom of the pond. Every muscle ached with the effort. He was so weak that a dozen kicks of his feet exhausted him. He paused, then moved toward the surface, kicking weakly again, his need for air coming within seconds rather than long minutes. When he surfaced, the sun burned into his black eyes. He felt dizzy. But his recovery, once begun, could not be stopped.

He did not yet know it, but the epidemic had liberated him. It had given him a new world of freedom. No longer would there be the pressure of intruders at the edges of his territory. They were all gone. He swam and drifted the full length of the pond during this day and met no other muskrat. He floated and dived, enjoying the luxury of his recovering strength.

He knew nothing of the effects of the drought on the pond, but he was to benefit from them. The heat had grown during his sickness, burning the color from plants and grasses. Planarian worms starved as the pond shrank, but they did not die. Instead, they regressed to their newborn state and would not grow adult organs or regain their mature size until the drought was over. Many creatures in the pond began laying eggs which did not hatch. These eggs were designed to survive unhatched beyond the reach of the drought. The minnows, who must feed on creatures hatching from such eggs, faced starvation. Datra, making hardly any effort, found and ate them as he drifted. The minnows became smaller each day. They consumed their own bodies to live. Then they began dying, their corpses caught in pond weeds or driven ashore. Datra swam among the helpless minnows and their rich flesh was medicine for his recovering strength.

Gradually he grew strong. The cattails towered ten feet above him. In their mysterious jungles, Datra moved among the debris of other hunters: fish skeletons, piles of amphibian bones, clusters of marsh bird feathers, piles of shellfish. The nests of meadow mice built in the jungles just above the level of the water trembled as he approached and methodically tore them to pieces. The cattails were infested with weevils, and birds feasted on the insects. Datra walked across the mud of the shallows, leaving his track of four feet and the unbroken dragline of his tail.

He was free from the need to fight. He had plenty of food, and no muskrat threatened his territory. But the memory of the sickness and the attack of the minks haunted his nights. He slept poorly, awakened many times by imagined sounds outside the lodge. When a mink screamed, he shivered in terror. Sometimes at night he surfaced near the lodge and watched the trees standing along the edge of the pond, as still as sentinels. Fox cubs yapped in the distance. Dark wings fled across the moon.

In his imagination the pond turned over again. Datra felt his body prickling with fright. He imagined a mink hissing in his ear. A branch splashed onto the pond. Bright white lights stabbed his eyes. He imagined he was sick again. Digging sounds roared in his head. Finally, unable to stand his delusions any longer, he swam desperately for the shore.

Instead of heading for the marsh, or his lodge, Datra took to the northern woods. Instead of staying in a familiar world, he chose the alien one. In this strange world, he moved clumsily, noisily. He was making no careful journey in search of a new and safer place. Rather, he was embarked on an expedition born of desperation. His life had been so thoroughly upset by disaster that now he scarcely knew what he was doing.

All his great strengths, his swimming, his diving and building abilities, were stripped from him in the forest. His fear of flying things, which kept him wary and alert at the pond, terrified him here. He faced a clearing in the dark woods. Tall, bleached grasses murmured with the sounds of insects. He was preparing to cross the clearing when high-pitched cries sounded overhead. He rushed headfirst into the thick grasses. Through their network above him he saw two hawks descending in great, broad-winged swoops. A squirrel dashed through the branches of a nearby oak. The hawks came down quickly and the sound of their wings was like a soft, menacing wind. The squirrel, far faster than her enemies, spiraled the tree and jumped from branch to branch, but always the hawks were on either side of her. Datra heard the flailing wings, the harsh breaths, and the scratch of claws. The squirrel ran well; she jumped magnificently, but her last sound was a gasp as she was gripped in the lungs in the middle of one great jump to eternity.

Datra remained still in the thick grasses until the hawks had gone. Then he ran, he loped, he jumped, and did not stop until he had wedged himself as deep as he could go inside a jumble of rocks in a dry stream bed. The forest was silent; the only sound now was the beating of his pumping heart.

Datra had penetrated the woods so deeply that he was uncertain of the position of the pond. He had followed stream beds, climbed hills, and descended them. But he had come too far to remember all his changes of direction. He did remember, though, that he had traveled against the currents of streams. So now he walked and swam with the trickles of water still running through the woods. He felt a great aloneness and was puzzled that he should be so far from home. He would never understand the reason for his journey. He had responded automatically to the signal to move that muskrats get when their lives becomes unbearable. Now, though, he wanted only to see the pond again.

In the next days his progress was faulty and uncertain. He saw blackbirds clattering past, headed south, as he was. Cicadas thickened and roared in the trees. He hid while a family of playful jays mobbed a squirrel.

Then one night, while sheltering deep inside a rock crevice, he heard the sound of dogs barking. A flurry of footsteps came near, then the sounds of voices and the frantic baying of dogs who had sighted, or scented, their prey. Shadows flickered inside his refuge as flashlights played in the forest outside. Datra huddled down, trying to make himself as small as possible.

He saw nothing of the young raccoons hidden all around him. But when the dogs found one of the youngsters and killed it, the snap of their biting teeth, their pants and gasps of excitement were so close they seemed about to push through the entrance of his refuge. At dawn the forest was still except for the pure cries of birds. He emerged cautiously. Then he ran, jumping like a kangaroo over stones and sticks, running with absolute assurance, heading directly south, not caring whether he was seen or heard, running until he saw through the trees water flickering in the sun, leaping recklessly, and finally plunging into the security of his pond.

CHAPTER IX

The lodge was a mess. Only a ragged wreck remained above the water and its interior had been torn to pieces. When Datra swam inquiringly to its ruined side, he caught the faint odor of otter, an ancient enemy. The otters had been destructive on their other occasional visits to the pond, but such methodical leveling of the lodge was unusual. While Datra investigated, rain began to spatter around him.

Rain fell steadily as Datra quickly slipped back into his old routines. His long absence from the pond had upset a vital activity of the season. To survive the winter ahead, he must be well housed. Now he had little time to finish a lodge before the tumult of the fall season began.

As he worked rapidly to reconstruct the lodge, the face of the pond was touched by odd leaves pulled down by occasional restless winds from the surrounding trees. The fall of the leaves thickened. Soon they ran along the shores of the pond in rustling battalions. Datra worked on. He was aware that a great movement of creatures into the pond had begun, but he ignored them. All were seeking the same kind of refuge that he himself was building into the lodge.

When he swam in search of building material, he scattered gatherings of frogs floating together, as if contemplating their next move. One day they passed by him, thrusting themselves down into the deepest parts of the pond. Later, unseen by him, they would burrow into the mud of the bottom. Salamanders and toads came down from the woods and entered the pond. Tree frogs, climbing down from tall summer perches in the trees, worked their way into hiding places in rotten stumps at the edge of the pond.

Datra continued to build, his mouth filled with debris, as the lodge gradually grew back into its original form.

This was the time of the great owl, and his cry dominated the pond at night. This was a time of gatherings of redwings, uproarious congregations of grackles, and swelling flocks of crows. The big owl came to the pond to prey on these multitudes. Once, swimming unwarily in a night so black he could scarcely see, Datra felt his back struck by a sharp lance of fire. He flipped and hurled himself underwater. The great owl turned at the end of the pond and made another sweep low across the water, his great night-seeing eyes seeking another glimpse of the swimming muskrat. But Datra was on the bottom, his head buried in the mud.

One evening Datra stood, apprehensive and still, on top of his lodge, listening to the distant sound of the owl's cry. It had the softness of a dove's voice, but it was so deep, so deceptive in its loudness, that it carried with it a kind of sinister and deadly strength. Datra shivered, and dived.

And on some nights, when the crows were roosting to the west, Datra surfaced to the sounds of thrashing wings and screaming birds. He heard the chokes and grunts as the great horned owl made carnage of the helpless and hysterical birds.

The creatures of the pond and the land surrounding it must move with Datra, must find new places to escape the winter, or die. Millions of tiny creatures, the spiders, bugs, beetles, caterpillars and larvae of many other insects, began to migrate vertically. They came down from the tips of the tallest trees, down from shrubs, down from hiding places in bark, and headed for the soil and cover of the falling leaves. As they came down, the wind took some of them and bore them away. The waters of the pond were specked with their falling bodies. Datra, hard at work, witnessed their fall, sometimes with hungry interest when his mouth was not full of building material.

Earthworms, feeling the first chills of the changing season, dug deeper into the ground to stay under the reach of the frost. Nymphs in the pond moved into the deepest water and buried themselves in mud. Snails moved in a body away from the dangerous shores while whirligig beetles and water striders dropped down the stems of plants, each cold day putting them inches deeper so that they would soon be at the bottom.

The movement of the season spread. Newts, compelled by the migration fever, moved on the warmer days and held their positions on the cold days. Some swam upstream away from the pond and tried to conquer rapid currents over stones. Hundreds of them lined the banks of the pond, waiting for the moment when the real cold would begin. Then they could fall to the bottom with the plants to which they were clinging.

As Datra swam deeply in search of lodge material, just above the muddy bottom of the pond, he saw the roads made by thousands of migrant snails. The tracks led downhill, down toward the bottom, down among piles of summer-constructed debris, of decaying leaves and broken stems.

Datra became more aware of the changing season with each passing day, and he worked feverishly. He was fixed in his notion of building a lodge the same way as he had the old one. This meant he must gather an enormous amount of material. He had always lived on a larger scale than most of the other muskrats, and he could not now change his habits, despite the pressure of time.

All around him other creatures of the pond were also at work, but in different ways. Many of them fattened, or grew denser coats, or changed the functioning of their livers, or contracted their stomachs, or expelled all excess water from their bodies, or changed their plumages, or used a thousand other devices to ready themselves for winter.

At one point during Datra's work, heavy rains sharply lifted the level of the pond and built roaring masses of sound against the trees. He felt the half-completed lodge move. He had fastened the new home to the bottom by adding small pieces of mud to the old foundations, building a broad circle as he sought to form a strong island. He reinforced the mud with lengths of dried cattail stems and leaves. Once his lodge had reached the surface of the water, he had started to roof it over with a mixture of vegetation and mud. But in his haste he had worked with a minimum of materials. Now the pouring rain and the rising pond waters were upsetting his work. The water soaked through the roof. Part of it fell in on him and he was left floundering in a mass of choking mud and debris. Then the rest of the roof came down and he was trapped in the stuff. He tried to nose his way out to the underwater exit, but in the dark his probing snout found no sign of the tunnel. He burrowed down twice, found only dense, sticky mud, and eventually, in disgust, he burst his way through the collapsing roof into the open air.

The drumming rain thickened and made the surface of the pond opaque. Datra dived again and came up under the lodge through his submarine exit and heard the sound of water gurgling higher into the body of the lodge. He remembered the great flood of the spring, when he had been driven from the safety of his lodge.

He returned to the surface and felt the power of this rain.

The sound of it filled his ears. Before dusk the water had washed deeply into the lodge, and when he managed to force his way back into the wreckage of the main chamber, he found water pouring through its damaged roof. The lodge was lost, he knew that now, but he still was reluctant to go into flood waters. He turned and felt his way back down in the darkness to the exit tunnel. Already it was beginning to disintegrate and he pushed his way past rubbish into open, deep water. When he surfaced, he felt himself caught by conflicting currents. In the tiny light still available, he saw the darting forms of other creatures seeking new places. He headed for the deepest part of the pond and rested on the bottom, motionless, his great lungs holding precious oxygen while the rest of his body drew sparingly on it. Then, when his reserves were down to a minute, he slowly clawed his way upward toward the dark surface and into the perils of the storm.

At the surface all was confusion. The currents swept him along in a tangled mixture of tree branches, grasses, leaves, feebly swimming mice, dead and dying birds. Datra tried to swim north, as was his custom, toward the familiar territory of his food-hunting areas, where shelving banks and weed-choked shallows would give him a grip on vegetation, a place to hold until the flood's strength diminished.

But, turned many times back and forth by the current, his aim was fairly faulty. He was actually swimming west when he first heard the roaring of a stream. Now desperation turned to panic and he drew breath and dived again.

Once beneath the surface, he swam better but the pull of the current strengthened. He felt himself moving sideways, and turned to swim into the current, but he already knew that he had lost the fight.

Then he was flying through the water in a nightmare ride. No longer able to swim in one direction, he let himself go limp. He was jolted when he hit some obstruction and his spine twisted agonizingly. He bashed into a stone, struck a mass of clinging grasses, found himself on the surface, thrown into the air on the crest of a billow, then plunged deep into black water.

There was no sense or order in this mad world and Datra sucked in one gasp of water instead of air. He choked, moving his limbs feebly, mouth half-agape. His speed increased. With all control lost, his only hope was to be flung ashore at the edge of this roaring stream.

He plunged over an invisible waterfall, jarred bone and skull when he was dropped onto a gravel bottom, spun over a dozen times, twirled in a whirlpool, then twisted the other way as he turned into a backwater. There, dizzy and disoriented, he tried to swim without notion of direction. By luck he swam away from the force of the stream and so reached the shelving shore. He crawled feebly up to the nearby trees and buried himself in protective leaves.

When Datra cautiously raised his snout into the pallid air of morning, he looked into an alien country. Pine woods surrounded him. White fleecy clouds moved silently beyond the reach of the highest trees. The smell of death was pun-

gent in his nostrils. Datra shivered. He knew he must find shelter, but not here, not in these malevolent woods. He moved out of reach of the trees, avoiding the body of a dead crow, and fearfully scurried west. Unlike other forest creatures, the crow or raccoon or owl, Datra had no knowledge of the burned church, or the burned farmhouse which lay to the west. He had no way of knowing that men had been there once. All he understood was the need for shelter, away from the pine woods. When he reached the ruins of the burned church, he found a hole along the base of the building's foundations and pushed inside.

Vaguely familiar smells touched his nostrils. There were strangers in here somewhere, but he was not frightened. He got no smell of raccoon or fox. Rather, this was the smell of creatures like himself. The glow of light from the entrance hole paled behind him as he passed through other holes dug in loose earth, pushing his way through rotten wood until he was under the burned floor of the vanished church. Scurrying sounds raced beyond him. Squeaking voices sounded in the gloom. Datra did not know it, but he had entered the world of the wood rat, a rodent like himself, who had chosen to live in the woods rather than in the water. The wood rats were smaller than he, less fierce and determined, and quite unable to contest his entry into their home.

And then, without warning, he heard the barking of dogs, the thunder of footsteps above him. He crouched down fearfully, hearing the snuffling hounds, the heavy footsteps of the men.

CHAPTER X

Datra trembled at the sound of the men's dogs. When they plunged clumsily through the shallows of the pond or bayed in the woods, he always sought the deepest shelter he could find. He was less afraid of the men, but the beams of their flashlights probing among the trees and the crash of their footsteps at the pond on quiet nights still terrified him. He could not know that his pond was a sanctuary where men must walk and hunt furtively, breaking their own laws.

Here, far from the pond, Datra was twenty times more vulnerable. This was truly man's territory where his dogs ran free. The footsteps pounded overhead, the gasping breaths of the dogs boomed and echoed in the dark space underneath as they sniffed at the burned floor. Datra remained motionless. When the sounds died away, he decided to leave.

He looked outside. There was no sign of man or dog. He started into the open and headed for a line of trees running along a distant stream. Just before he reached the trees, he heard heavy, pounding footsteps. Looking back, he saw a dog running silently behind him. He fled; great bounding leaps took him almost blindly among the trees. The sound of the dog's breath was so loud that he expected to feel teeth in his back at any moment. At the edge of the stream bed, he jumped from a rock, hurling himself blindly outward, not knowing that the dog's teeth chopped air just behind him. He hit the ground, rolled, and saw the dog blundering over the edge after him.

Datra's fall was lucky. He bounced down a rocky slope and with one final jump disappeared into the darkness of a crevice in the rocks. Down, down he fell, bouncing off the sides of the crevice until he hit water. It was shallow, but Datra knew he was safe.

The dog rolled down the sides of the crevice and Datra heard his frantic barking far above him. A second dog's voice joined in. Then came the sounds of men's voices. A rock clattered down and splashed into the water nearby. Datra remained absolutely still. After long minutes the sounds of dogs and men died away completely. But now Datra was cautious. He stayed motionless in the water for a day and a night.

The close escape from the dog put Datra in an agony of

indecision. The flood at the pond had upset his routines and triggered the urge to move. But this migration urge was modified by his fear of the dogs and by his experiences in the woods before the flood. Still, the urge, the restlessness, was too strong for him to turn back toward the pond. He waited in the moonlight near the base of a tree, whiskers trembling, waited for the next sign that would make him move. He must have shelter. He should have water. His urge was to go south, but the dogs always barked in the south and he understood what danger lay there.

He turned west into a gusting wind, and sniffed for the smell of water. He struggled through long grasses and stamped down a slope half-sheltered by trees, where the earth was damp and loose. Debris had collected there among some scattered stones. Datra began digging in the rich black earth.

He worked all night with the energy of silent desperation, and by morning his paws and muzzle were caked with black earth. A long ribbon of dark soil spilled from the burrow hole. He had dug down diagonally and then turned at right angles under a large stone. Beyond that, his digging stopped by a very large boulder, he had hollowed out his refuge chamber. Before dawn paled, he had spread some of the debris of his digging, kicking it among the leaves. He had dug some roots and put them in the chamber. He had even made a foray out into open country nearby, a farmer's field, and had picked two heads of corn. He found them delicious. He did not need to test whether it was safe to move by daylight. He knew immediately that here he must be nocturnal.

Over the ensuing days Datra prowled the cornfield. He watched for his enemies from the safety of piles of corn stalks. The sound of dogs passed and repassed by day and by night. Sometimes they stopped at the entrance to his burrow and thrust their big faces into the earth, whimpered, and dug a little. But always they passed on, their barks disappearing to the west.

Now Datra felt the first real touches of winter. Huddled in his new burrow, he remembered all his winters, remembered the ice working its way up through the floor of lodges he had built too low in the water, remembered waves beating against the walls of lodges built too high. He remembered entrance holes constructed too close to the water level and frozen solid in deep freezes. He remembered lodges with walls and ceilings too thin, the air inside suffocating in summer heat.

Now, he knew, young muskrats would be working hard at the pond to finish lodges amid the first crackle of ice. In his dreams he could see lodge after lodge rising clumsily out of the water. Many of these would not survive the gales and rains of the early winter. Some would collapse, or be swept away by moving ice. The late-building animals were always the most vulnerable, their choice of lodge places was only by accident. Most of them would be abandoned as the winter became tougher. Then their owners must beg entrance into larger and better founded lodges or make dubious migrations to other places.

Datra's memories of the pond became so strong that abruptly one midnight he roused himself, left his burrow, and set out in a dead run to the east. He swam across the stream which had saved him from the dog, leaped over rocks, ignored the cries of hunting owls, scampered in moonlight past the burned church and farmhouse, skirted the grove of pines where death lived. His feeling about the pond was now unbearable. All its seasons were vivid and affecting in his memory. As he ran, he imagined he saw the collecting of crows, the departure of redwings, the hunting mink. The visions shifted before his eyes so that he ached for a view of his natural home. He reached the pond at dawn, and dived.

He floated in the pond, the light growing around him, and his bones felt tired. Oddly, his senses of hearing and sight were made more acute by this feeling. He popped to the surface a dozen times and looked around the pond. Reminders of the flood were everywhere. The smashed cattails lay flat, and dead pond weeds littered the shore. Nothing moved. The only sound was the creaking of an old tree on the north shore.

Datra was old but he had never admitted it. He had fought hard to live and had not conceded defeat to the many forces seeking to kill him. His determination to live had kept him alive. He watched the creaking tree. It was old. The tree had fought too, but it had lost. Its plight had been signaled by the hammerings of woodpeckers, by the careful work of carpenter ants, by the burrowing of beetles, by fungus and termites.

Datra watched it and listened. The tree creaked. Beetles had dug through its body, creating a kind of buried empire of creatures. A labyrinth of tunnels and galleries grew as they ate the tree and sheltered within it. Years before, a pair of carpenter ants had mated and then flown off in search of a place to create a colony. They had drifted, light as thistledown in clear air, until they had crossed the pond and reached the maple. They had landed and entered it, dropping their wings as they crawled through a beetle's hole.

While the young Datra, just out of his mother's lodge, was fighting for a place in the pond, the carpenter ants were reaching deeper into the tree, hunting beetles and eating them, and tending their first youngsters, who would soon become nurses to new generations of ants. The branches of the maple still flourished green in the spring sun, but its heart had gone. It had no reserve now against the next high wind, the next stroke of lightning, the next plan of cunning men who knew that, at heart, the tree was dead.

In the days following his return to the pond, Datra met newcomers at its shores and drove them back. He evicted three muskrats from the half-rebuilt ruins of his lodge. He chased all intruders from his territory. He worked with a kind of frenzy that could not last. He had no hope of finishing the lodge before the first real freeze came, but a premonition, a fragile, growing fear, drove him on. Already the land around the pond lay under snow, and the shallows sparkled with a coat of thin ice on cold mornings.

One day, while he was swimming through thin ice with his mouth full of old reeds, a gun boomed nearby and Datra dropped the reeds. Above him he heard the frantic scrabbling and beating of wings in the creaking old maple. A crow, sick and old, had fallen and caught his foot in the fork of a branch. He cried out, but no other crow responded.

Datra headed for the half-finished lodge as the gun sounded again and a dog barked. Now his fragile fear was solid enough. Men were coming. Danger threatened the pond. He dived, but in mid-swim he surfaced again. More dogs barked. The crunch of men's feet sounded in the crusty snow.

Uncertain of what to do, Datra headed back toward the lodge. He lifted his muzzle out of the water and waited near the side of the lodge. The bird in the tree was silent. In the next moment the dogs arrived, dashing along the edge of the pond, and stopped, barking at the foot of the dead tree.

Datra was transfixed. He wanted to flee, but the memory of his past two flights stopped him. He wanted to bury himself in the lodge, but it wasn't finished. Instead, he watched the men come up to the tree, kick the dogs away, and drop their guns. A raccoon looked out from her refuge hole high in the tree. The men gripped the tree trunk and slowly began rocking it back and forth.

The movement of the tree galvanized Datra. He dived, came up underneath the lodge, and plunged into its unfinished main chamber. He lay down, curled his body, and tried to shut out the gush of images that shuttled through his head. Although his eyes were closed tight, he could not banish the sight of the stricken tree.

The snap of its breaking trunk sounded across the pond. The raccoon and the crow felt the maple falling. Datra

heard the crow's cry and the flop of wings as he tried to stop
his fall. He heard the raccoon scream as she braced herself
against the rim of her refuge hole and watched the ground
rushing up to meet her. The sounds were too frightening,
and Datra burst through the roof of his lodge. The hounds
howled, the men shouted, and with a tremendous crash the
tree landed on top of Datra. A great wave of water sprang
away to all corners of the pond.

Stunned, Datra saw nothing of the raccoon's escape from
the maple. She jumped from her hole just before the tree
struck, rolling herself into a tight ball, and tumbled away
from the fallen tree. Datra did not see the crow crash into
the water, his leg jolted loose from its trap by the force of
his fall. The terrified bird thrashed his way through the
encircling branches while the raccoon hurled herself at an
attacking hound.

Beneath the water, all Datra's fears had come true. He
tried to swim upward but was stopped by a crush of branches.
He tried to swim down, but nowhere in the darkness could
he find a place not blocked by the shattered wreckage of the
tree. A gun sounded so close that he was deafened. A dog
howled in pain. The water gurgled and moved around him
as he fought to claw a hole in his prison, but his strongest
efforts advanced him hardly a paw's length. He became more
and more frantic. Juices flowed in his body. He became
young in strength as he ripped and tore and inched forward.
Then he was free, rising swiftly to the surface. The debris
of the dead tree lay all around him. The dogs and the men

had gone. The shaken raccoon shivered on the southern shore. From the west came the solitary cry of a crow. Immense tiredness enveloped Datra. Now he knew he was old. The message had been given him. Now he knew he must make one last journey in search of that secure place which haunted his dreams. Now the pond belonged to younger muskrats.

He slipped away across the water. He let himself be carried by the outlet stream, and his pond dropped behind him, sinking slowly into its winter sleep.